FOR DAVID, MY HEART'S DESIRE

ACKNOWLEDGMENTS

It is a privilege to give my heartfelt thanks to Jodi Kreitzman,
my editor at Knopf, for her superb creative insights and her
unbounded passion for this project. Not only did she guide me
through the rascally wilderness of bookmaking, she taught
me much about grace and patience along the way.
I'm a better person for having worked with her these last two years.

Thanks again to Judy Blume. The whole journey began when
I met Margaret between the pages.

Jules Feiffer, Anna Paganelli, and Graham Salisbury
have been beacons along the way.

To the thousands of teenagers, librarians, parents, teachers, and
others who have visited Favorite Teenage Angstbooks on the Web
(www.grouchy.com/angst) and have written to me:
I agree! Books change our lives,
and—lucky me—you've changed mine. Thank you.

CONTENTS

Introduction **Cathy Young** 1

Rules for Love and Death **Ellen Wittlinger** 7

Who Hears the Fish Cry? **Norma Fox Mazer** 27

Driving Her Wild **Jennifer Armstrong** 51

The County Fair **Victor Martinez** 59

Loving Megan **Nancy Garden** 81

One Hot Second **Rachel Vail** 107

Someone Bold **Sarah Dessen** 127

Lorena **Jacqueline Woodson** 147

Team Men **Emma Donoghue** 161

Dawn **Rich Wallace** 181

A Kind of Music **Angela Johnson** 203

About the Editor 218

INTRODUCTION

SECRET CRUSHES. Awkward dates. Fumbled kisses. Shy glances. First love. First times.

You're in for a treat. Eleven brilliant, award-winning writers for teens dove deep into their hearts to explore the mysteries of desire. Here, in their stories, you'll taste desire's different flavors, see its true colors, and feel its knobby textures. You'll hear honesty, hope, struggle, and some delicious thoughts guaranteed to give rise to a blush or two.

Desire is utterly unpredictable. Elusive. Sometimes it's a whisper when it first awakens within us. Other times desire chooses the most awkward moment to steamroll us, leaving us flattened, confused, and forever changed. Desire drives us all a little crazy. Know the feeling?

I can tell you for a fact that desire first wreaked havoc on my life on January 12, 1975. That was the day I abandoned my diary's page-a-day format and wrote eight full pages about Ray, the boy who sat next to me in fifth grade. I scrawled like the wind, plotting every detail of what our first kiss would be like. In the hall near the lockers . . . or no . . . it would be underneath the shady tree by the track. He would take my hand, pull me close, and cover my cheeks with kisses. Time would whoosh away, and my legs would melt. He'd have to steady me, of course. Then I would feel his lips against mine, warm and sweet.

Unfortunately, my hormone-fueled imagination was more developed than Ray's. Not yet the romantic hero of my dreams, he responded to my blushing smiles with goofy faces, complete with handcrafted rubber-cement boogers hanging from his nostril.

Thankfully, desire doesn't need a perfect object to work its magic. As you'll discover from the stories in this collection, desire takes on many forms after that first stir. It takes root within—shaping our moods, filling us with hopeful jitters, tripping us in the hallway (especially when we're trying hard to be extra-smooth), electrifying new territories in our bodies.

Meet Krystal—the brave, misunderstood protagonist in Norma Fox Mazer's "Who Hears the Fish Cry?" Wearing a jaded snarl like lipstick camouflage, Krystal hides the vibrant energy percolating inside her—until she meets Tyler, a skinny blond guy who actually seems to "get" her, odd music tastes and all. Through Mazer's sensitive storytelling, we come to see that our romantic desires often are about much more than sex. . . . Sometimes they lead us down a path toward healing.

In "Someone Bold," Sarah Dessen explores how being desired (and being undesirable) can inspire a whole new way of seeing ourselves. Now that Angela has lost weight and gained new confidence, she takes a hard look at the people in her life who have betrayed her. What she discovers may surprise you.

In a delightful twist, Nancy Garden introduces us to Penny, a girl whose biggest problem is not that she's attracted to girls but that she may be attracted to the *wrong* girl. "Loving Megan" tracks Penny's race to be noticed and befriended by the beautiful, confident Megan.

In Victor Martinez's lush, bittersweet story "The County Fair," we see desire evolve from simple to complex during the course of just one date. At first it feels as unencumbered and fresh as Roybal's love for Carol's smile and the swish of her ponytail. Soon, though, we see how easily desire can be burdened by race, social status, and family expectations.

Tangled tongues, saliva, and warm breath? If you think about it, you have to admit that kissing is very, very weird. Mallory has the real dirt on kissing, boys, and moments of ninth-grade passion in Rachel Vail's "One Hot Second."

Jennifer Armstrong holds nothing back in her sizzling story "Driving Her Wild." Its unexpected ending reminds us that sometimes the crush and that wonderful ache inside are not *just* about the object of desire but also about stretching toward maturity or a new sense of self.

In "Lorena," Jacqueline Woodson tells a heart-wrenching tale of love lost. In passages that move like poetry, we come to learn how Natalie and Lorena were split apart. The feelings are complicated, shattering, and painful. As Natalie faces her grief, the truth unfolds.

Do you have a friend who started dating before you? In "Rules for Love and Death," Ellen Wittlinger describes the awkward feelings of betrayal and envy that develop when Casey sees one of her close friends moving ahead without her. In the end, though, we're not sure exactly who has been left behind as Casey begins to appreciate love in a whole new way after one of her classmates dies.

You'll meet Jon and Davy in Emma Donoghue's "Team Men." Their relationship plays out on the soccer field, where the rough-and-tumble of sports gives way to a connection between them. Haunting and visceral, Donoghue's story touches on so many different kinds of desire—between family members and between friends.

Rich Wallace, a master at finding meaning in the middle of the game, tackles lust head-on in "Dawn." At a summer workshop for creative teens, Ronny finds himself smitten with a fellow writer named Dawn. He may have met his match, though, because Dawn exudes such an intoxicating mix of intelligence and grace that he's not sure if they're even in the same league. How will she respond to his brazen moves? The provocative scene that unfolds is unforgettable.

Close your eyes and imagine how desire might sound if it were a song. Feel that rising beat? That's what you'll experience when you dive into Angela Johnson's sexy "A Kind of Music." Johnson's prose echoes the rhythm of the heart as she tells the story of a girl discovering inner strength and the magic of first love.

I'm breathless! Here are eleven stories that celebrate teenage desire—provocative, honest, sometimes hilarious, sometimes heartbreaking, always stirring. Each of the fine writers in this collection honors the power of desire to push us forward into the unknown, to help us grow. Desire aches. Desire burns. And, thankfully, it blooms.

Cathy Young

RULES FOR LOVE

AND DEATH

ELLEN WITTLINGER

THE NEWS hit the high school Monday morning before the end of first period: Danny Bommarito had been killed in a car wreck Sunday night on Route 55 on his way home from Nicole Nesbit's house. As soon as Mr. Simonson announced it over the P.A. system, somebody started screaming in the hallway outside my geometry class. Ms. West put her hand over her mouth and leaned against the chalkboard while Mr. S. said that any friends of Danny's who were upset could leave class to talk to a counselor or the school nurse.

I bet Danny didn't know how many friends he had. In about a minute there were throngs of kids moving through the hallway, holding on to each other, sobbing like mad. Since Danny was a senior and most of the kids in my geometry class are only sophomores, hardly any of us knew him that well, but there were a few girls crying, and Will Jasper, who was on the football team with Danny, put his head down on his desk. I had never spoken a word to Danny Bommarito—at least, not out loud—but I had intended to, eventually. As soon as I figured out what to say.

Danny was in my study hall last year. He sat with the other juniors and seniors who did things: Peer Leaders, International Relations Club, student government. He was not just a jock— he did everything. If I got there early enough to get a seat at the right table, I could spend most of the period watching him without anybody noticing. I especially loved watching him laugh at jokes. Sometimes I even snickered along with him, which made the kids at my table stare at me like I was possessed. He had a really happy laugh that kind of exploded out of him.

When the bell rang, Danny would lean back in his chair and stretch out before he got moving, like school didn't rule him the way it did the rest of us. One time I stayed sitting in my seat too while everybody else grabbed their books and stampeded out of there. Suddenly Danny turned his head and looked right at me, like he'd known I was there.

"Hey," he said, and gave me a wink. That's all. "Hey" and a wink. Then he pulled himself out of his chair and went to catch up with one of his friends. I couldn't believe it. He knew I was there; he saw me; he spoke to me; he winked.

I went over and over it in my mind—it seemed like we had a secret now, Danny and I. Isn't that what a wink means? Or maybe it meant, I know you watch me. That might be okay too . . . if he knew I was interested. . . . But the year was almost over by then, and there wasn't really time for another wink.

At the beginning of this year I made my friend Violet go with me to a few Peer Leaders meetings, although I didn't tell her why. She had a boyfriend already, and I thought it might seem childish to her that I was following around some guy I barely knew. I didn't realize Danny's girlfriend, Nicole, was president of Peer Leaders. Ugh. They constantly found excuses to touch each other, like it was normal to give somebody a neck massage every time they blinked. I could never get up the nerve to speak to him, so I don't know if he remembered me from study hall or not. I was working on a question I could ask him, but then Vi and I quit the group when we found out the freshmen and sophomores had to do fund-raising.

"Not me," Violet said. "I'm in high school! I'm not selling candy bars door-to-door like some second grader!"

It's not like Danny Bommarito was the only good-looking upperclassman; he was just the one who seemed right to me. I don't know how to explain it, but when I heard him laugh, I'd get chills down my back. He had dark wavy hair that was always a little too long in the front—not perfect, you know, but perfect. And he seemed like a guy who'd be nice to you, if you ever actually knew him.

So when Mr. Simonson said there was this car crash last night . . . well, it couldn't be true because I never even had a chance to talk to Danny Bommarito . . . and I was in love with him.

In a few minutes Mr. Simonson was back on the air: "It's clear to me that it will be difficult to conduct regular classes today in light of the tragedy that has befallen us." That's the way he talks. "I am dismissing classes for the remainder of the day. However, I urge those of you who need comfort to seek out our excellent staff here at the school. . . ." He ended by begging us to drive carefully, but by that time we were halfway to our lockers and nobody was listening anymore.

I stared into my locker, but I didn't know what to take out of it. Ms. West hadn't even given us any homework yet—there was nothing to do. A group of freshman girls huddled together on the floor nearby, getting in everybody's way. They were consoling each other and trying to squeeze out a few tears. One of them kept ripping tissues out of a little plastic package and passing them to the others. God, they probably wouldn't be able to pick Danny out of a lineup.

"Casey! Can you believe this?" Violet came tearing around the corner. "It's not even nine o'clock yet and we're out of school! We should go someplace and do something!"

I shrugged halfheartedly. "Don't you want to hang with Burt?" Vi has been my best friend since kindergarten, but last year she also began to be Burt Baldwin's girlfriend, and it definitely got in the way of our friendship. We could never make plans until she'd checked with Burt to see what he wanted to do. She said rule number one was: Never screw over a girlfriend for a guy, unless you're in love with the guy. Then, apparently, anything is permissible. And of course Violet is in love.

She gave me a little tap on the back. "Don't be like that. I don't always hang with Burt. Besides, I just saw him and he says he's going back home to sleep."

"Not a bad idea," I said.

"Casey, this is a free day! We have to do something. It's like a present!"

Is that what it was like? How thoughtful of Danny to give us all a present. Even before I slammed my locker and started hightailing it for an exit, the tears began to creep down my cheeks. Violet was behind me, so she didn't notice right away.

"Why are you running?" She caught up with me as I headed out the back cafeteria door and almost fell over a girl lying motionless facedown on the bottom step. My God, had everybody been in love with Danny Bommarito?

There weren't many people coming out this way—it was the exit to the teachers' parking lot, and they were probably still inside meeting in small groups, all their hands over all their mouths. They probably knew all the details by now: where exactly it had happened, whether anybody saw it, who else got hurt, whose fault it was. I kept imagining Danny's green Honda flipped over on its back like a turtle, wheels spinning. I tried not to think where that meant Danny had been. Trapped inside the car? Thrown out onto the highway? Had he known he was going to die? Thinking about it made me put my hand over my mouth.

I made it to the corner where the trees start before Violet caught sight of my face.

"Are you crying?"

I wasn't making a sound—no sniffing, no hiccuping, nothing. I just let the silly water leak out silently.

"I didn't even think you knew Danny Bommarito!" Violet said. "Did you?"

I shook my head. "No, but I might have someday."

"What, you mean, like, you had a thing for him?"

I sighed. "Sort of."

Violet put her arm around my shoulder. She actually is a good friend when she's available. "Why didn't you tell me? I didn't even know!"

I swiped at the tears with the sleeve of my jacket. "It wasn't like you and Burt. But I thought it might be someday."

"I can't believe you didn't tell me this!"

I shrugged and gave a mucusy sniff, wishing I didn't sound so pathetic. "You're always so busy with—"

"I wish you'd stop saying that, Casey. We're still best friends—we're supposed to tell each other everything." Rule number two.

"There wasn't anything to tell. I just thought . . . I thought I'd talk to Danny someday, and . . . I don't know. He winked at me once. I just thought I'd get to talk to him." I could feel another downpour building behind my eyes.

Violet sucked in her breath. "You really liked him, didn't you?" I nodded and she hugged my shoulder tighter. "Oh, poor Casey! He is really cute. *Was*, I mean. God, I'm glad I didn't know him very well. It would be awful to have a friend who died young like that. It gives me goose bumps to think of it."

We stopped at the corner of Edgewood and Harrison and shivered, even though it was a warm Indian-summer day. I found a half-used tissue in my pocket and blew my nose. "Where are we going? Home or downtown?"

"Well, if you feel like it, could we go to the Pancake Palace and get some breakfast? I didn't have time to eat before I left home this morning. And there's something I want to talk to you about too. If you're okay." She gave me a slippery little grin and I had an idea what the topic was going to be. The last thing I was in the mood for this morning was tales of weekend lust in Burt's family room while Burt's family was somewhere else. But what choice did I have? Violet is my best friend. There are rules, you know.

We got a booth in the back corner so we could have some privacy. It was amazing how many other kids from school showed up. I guess grief makes you hungry. I ordered the special—two scrambled eggs, bacon, home fries, and a biscuit—while Violet, who hadn't already eaten a bowl of cereal this morning, ordered a cup of coffee and an English muffin.

"I thought you were hungry," I said. "You aren't getting nuts about your weight again, are you?"

"Don't worry so much. It's just hard to eat when you feel like this."

"Like what?"

She sucked in her breath and fluttered her hands in front of her chest to indicate that they were ready for takeoff, I guess. Vi can be a real drama queen. She likes to give you a big buildup before she tells you anything, which makes even ordinary stuff seem important. I don't have that talent, or maybe I just don't think anything that happens to me is important.

"What?" I repeated.

Violet leaned across the table to whisper to me. "That's what I wanted to talk to you about. I'm so excited."

"Why? Tell me, already."

The slippery grin returned. "We did it. Last night!" She spoke so quietly I had to read her lips, but then, the words were pretty simple to understand.

It's not like I was shocked or anything. I knew they'd been heading for it—Burt, especially, had been heading for it. Violet had been changing her mind practically every day: Do it; don't do it; do it. I guess she'd finally made up her mind.

But on the other hand, I *was* shocked. This was Violet, who I'd known since forever, who took dancing lessons with me at Ms. Patty's, who slept in my bunk with me at Camp Nashatoga on the nights the counselors told ghost stories, who went with me the first time I visited my father after he moved out, who never told her mother it was me who gave her that botched haircut in the seventh grade. It was bad enough she had a boyfriend and I didn't—but now she'd taken it one giant step further. Into the mysterious territory of sex: a faraway land to which I'd certainly never be able to follow her. I wasn't even sure I wanted to.

"Can you believe it?" she said. "I wasn't going to, but then, I don't know, nobody's ever home at Burt's, and all of a sudden there didn't seem to be a reason not to."

"You had a few hundred reasons last week," I reminded her. "Like whether you were in love or not, for one."

"I decided I am," she said firmly.

Just then the waitress brought big white plates, mine heaped with greasy food that didn't seem so appetizing anymore. I wished I liked coffee so at least I'd have that in common with Violet.

"Are you mad at me? Do you think it was wrong?" Violet dumped two packets of Sweet'n Low into her cup.

I shrugged. "It's your decision." All of a sudden I had this vision of the two of them lying together naked on some scratchy old brown couch with squeaky springs. God, Violet had seen Burt Baldwin naked. Ugh! It was one thing to hang out with the guy, kiss him and stuff, but to actually sleep with him? He was so . . . lumpy. And he was trying to grow this skimpy little mustache. And he hardly ever even spoke to me. If I was going to sleep with somebody, he would have to be . . . well, Danny Bommarito. But when I thought that, a hot nausea swept over me. I had to say something to Violet, though, so I said, "You did use something, didn't you?" I guess my voice carries.

Violet ducked her head. "Casey! Keep it down! I'm not advertising it!"

"Sorry."

"Of course we used something. Burt had condoms."

Condoms. Plural.

All of a sudden I remembered the time Vi and I found some condoms in her older brother's room and filled them up like water balloons. We were only about ten at the time. They looked so funny we called them our hot-dog toys and laughed until we practically peed our pants.

Violet grabbed my hands and leaned over the table to get my attention back. "It was wonderful, Case. Now I really understand what love is. Burt was so sweet. He kept asking me if it felt good."

I swallowed. I did actually want to know about this—I wanted the information from someone who'd been there, just in case I was ever faced with a sudden journey myself. Still, it was embarrassing to have to ask. "Did it feel good?"

I could tell she was glad I wanted to know. "I wish I could explain it to you," she said, her face dreamy. I remembered one time she'd told me, "If you love somebody, it should show on your face." Violet's face looked more like somebody appreciating a hot-fudge sundae.

"Well, try," I said.

"It's not like anything else."

"Really? I thought it would be just like volleyball."

She ignored me. "It's like floating on clouds or something. It's just . . . wonderful!"

Floating on clouds? Like those babies in the toilet-paper commercial? I needed one or two details, just in case. "Did he get on top, like in the movies?"

She nodded.

"And it didn't hurt or anything? When he . . . you know . . . put it in?"

Violet smiled. "You don't think about things like that, if it hurts or not. You're just thinking about how much you love him, and how you want to hold on to him and keep him warm inside you forever!"

Sounded sort of like a broken toaster to me. Enough. These weren't details anyway. They were advertisements.

"Will you go to the funeral with me?" I asked.

"What?" Violet was far away, dreaming of her love. I guess you forget about death in the land of toast. "You want to go to Danny Bommarito's funeral? Why? Funerals are awful—besides, you didn't really know him."

Right then I came up with a rule of my own, but I didn't tell Violet: If you love somebody, you should show up at their funeral. "Well, I'm going," I said solemnly. Violet frowned.

"They'll probably let us out of school to go," I said. "Like they did in middle school when that girl died of leukemia."

"That's true." She thought about it as she snitched half a piece of my bacon. "Did he really wink at you?"

I nodded.

Violet returned from Loveland to earth. She looked deep into my eyes. "Well, you can't go by yourself, Casey. I'll go with you so you can just fall apart if you want to. I'll be there to hold you up."

But when Wednesday afternoon rolled around and we signed out of school with a throng of other, mostly older kids, I thought Violet might be the one who'd need holding up. I'd gone to look for her and found her standing in front of her locker having an argument with Burt. I waited in a doorway down the hall, but I could still hear them.

"Don't be like that, Burt," Violet said in a begging voice I hated.

"Hey, go if you want to. I don't care. But I'm not wasting my afternoon at some crying-fest funeral for some kid I don't even know."

"The point is, you know Casey. We'd be there to support her."

"I don't know Casey. She's your friend." Burt was scanning the passersby, giving big grins and thumbs-ups to kids he was willing to admit he knew.

Violet gave up. "Fine. Are you coming over tonight?"

"Why don't you come by my house? Everybody'll be out again." He was looking at her now, his arm creeping around her side to lie on her butt. I felt like knocking it off myself, but Vi let it stay.

"I have a paper to write," she said, but she didn't sound too sorry about it.

"So? Write it afterwards!"

"No! Burt! Just because . . ." And then her voice got too low for me to make out, but my imagination filled in the blanks.

Burt looked angry. "God, Vi, I didn't think you'd turn into such a priss afterwards. What's wrong with you? How about this? You call me when you don't have so much homework to do." He stalked off, shaking his head; Vi slammed her locker door and then slumped against it. Was this what happened after you floated on clouds together?

"Hey, Vi!" I called, like I'd just shown up. "The bus is here." She took a deep breath before she joined me.

The school had chartered a decrepit bus to take those of us who didn't have a car or a ride to the funeral. It was too old to have seat belts, which seemed pretty lousy considering where we were going and why. Violet and I chose a front seat as the bus filled up with the JV football team and a bunch of the younger cheerleaders.

"I don't even know any of these kids," Violet said. "I bet they think it's weird we're going."

"It's not weird. Anybody can go to a funeral."

"Yeah, but we didn't know this guy," Violet reminded me in a grouchy whisper.

"We could have known him," I said. Anyway, I felt sure that by watching him all those months I knew the real Danny a lot better than most of these second-stringers did.

Violet rolled her eyes at me, scratched the back of her head, then stuck her hand down her turtleneck jersey to rearrange her bra. She was so fidgety she was making me jumpy too.

"What's the matter with you?"

"I feel all itchy," Violet said. "I think I'm allergic to funerals."

"I've never even been to one before," I admitted.

"You haven't? God, my mother is always dragging me in to say good-bye to every ancient relative who bites the dust."

"Violet!"

"I'm sorry, but I hate funerals. They're so fake. You stand there looking at this person you barely knew lying in a big silver bullet, all powdered and dressed up for the big trip to nowhere." She shivered. "People act like they're so upset, even when they aren't. It's a funeral rule. When my great-aunt died last year, everybody came up and shook her daughter's hand and said how terrible it was and how they'd all miss dear old Polly. Nobody liked this woman—she was the crab of the family. She had a cocker spaniel she trained to bite people. But as soon as she's out from underfoot, they're all crying about it. It gives me the creeps."

"This funeral won't be like that. Everybody *will* be upset."

Violet sighed. "Oh yeah. That'll make it a lot better."

"You know what I've been thinking about?"

"God knows."

I wasn't sure I should actually mention this to Violet, but the coincidence of it kept occurring to me. "You slept with Burt Sunday night, right?"

"Shh!"

"Sunday?" I whispered.

"Yes!"

"I keep thinking, you and Burt were probably doing it when

Danny had the accident. He probably died while you were making love for the first time. Isn't that weird?"

"Casey! God, you're freaking me out!"

"I don't mean it that way. I just mean, there was this terrible event happening at the same time that a good thing was beginning. In the same town. It just seems weird that I know about both things."

"It seems weird that you thought of it like that. Sex is nothing like death."

"They're both life-changing experiences. Especially death, I guess. But sex changes you too, doesn't it? You're not the same afterwards."

"That's the truth." Violet bent forward in the seat, her arms hugging her stomach. "Could we just not talk for a few minutes? This whole funeral thing is making me nauseous."

There was no room to sit down by the time the bus unloaded us at the church, so we stood in the back not far from the closed casket, which was on a wheeled cart surrounded by Danny's football teammates. They all had on dark suits and ties, so they were hardly recognizable as the same guys who shoved each other around in the halls at school. I had to look away from their faces as they wheeled the casket up the aisle to the front of the church. Some of them had tears rolling down their cheeks already. When I saw that, it hit me like a punch in the gut: This was real—Danny Bommarito was on the big trip to nowhere.

I couldn't actually hear too much of the service because there was a lot of crying going on. I cried too—it was almost impossible not to when everybody else was, but I wasn't feeling as heartbroken or cheated as I had on Monday when I first found out. I was actually having a hard time remembering exactly what Danny Bommarito looked like. Violet managed to stay dry by scowling at the bald head of the man in front of us.

When the minister was done speaking, the organ music blasted out of the ceiling speakers and the pallbearer team started rolling the casket back down the aisle. Behind them came a couple who must have been Danny's parents, and a younger sister—the father was in the middle with an arm around both females. All of them had swollen faces and red eyes. And then I saw who was coming next: Nicole Nesbit, Danny's girlfriend, one parent on either side of her, holding her up.

I watched her come closer. The president of the Peer Leaders couldn't seem to pick up her feet and kept stumbling on the carpet. Her mouth sagged open as if she didn't have the strength to keep it closed, and her eyes were swollen shut like two raw, red clamshells. Even her hair—Nicole Nesbit's beautiful dark hair—hung alongside her cheeks in damp, lanky hunks. When she passed me, I could hear how her breathing made a rasping noise in her chest; I could see she wasn't even inside herself. If you love somebody, it should show on your face.

"I have to sit down," I whispered to Violet, clutching her arm. She lurched to attention; this was the job she'd signed up for. Some of the people in the back rows had left through side doors, so Violet steered me to an empty pew and eased me into it like I was breakable. For a minute I had trouble breathing.

"It was too hard for you, wasn't it? God, Casey, I didn't know you loved him so much!" I looked up at her, my mouth open to explain, but nothing came out. Violet began to cry.

"I feel so stupid now," she said, slumping down next to me, holding my hand. "All that crap about being in love with Burt. That's how I wanted to feel, but it wasn't real, like . . . like this." Now she was really sobbing and everybody was respectfully averting their eyes. "It wasn't wonderful. It was weird and embarrassing and I don't care if we never do it again!"

Miraculously my voice returned. "Really? No clouds?" I asked, digging in my purse for tissues.

"I guess Burt made it to the clouds, but I sure didn't," she said, shuddering and mopping up her face. "I slept with him to find out if I loved him or not. I guess I got my answer."

We sat there by ourselves until the church was almost empty. Violet, not in love with Burt Baldwin. Me, not in love with Danny Bommarito.

About Ellen Wittlinger

Though she is a published poet and graduate of the Iowa Writers' Workshop, it wasn't until Ellen Wittlinger had children of her own and became a children's librarian that she thought of writing for young adults. Her first novels, *Lombardo's Law* and *Noticing Paradise*, earned rave reviews, but she is best known for her third novel, *Hard Love*. Among its numerous awards, *Hard Love* won a Lambda Literary Award and was named a Michael Printz Honor Book, an ALA Best Book for Young Adults, an IRA Young Adults' Choice, a *Booklist* Editors' Choice, and a *Bulletin* Blue Ribbon Book. She followed that success with *What's in a Name*, also an ALA Best Book for Young Adults and a *Bulletin* Blue Ribbon Book as well as a Massachusetts Book Award winner, *Gracie's Girl,* and *Razzle*. Over the years Ellen has taught writing courses at North Shore Community College in Beverly, Massachusetts, and Emerson College in Boston.

When asked to recall her own first crush, she writes, "I used to adore Mike, the hunky boy who lived across the street from me from the time I was eleven until I was about fourteen. I would sit at the window of my living room and stare at the blue curtains in his bedroom window, hoping to see them move or a shadow pass by them. I especially liked playing 'Johnny Angel' (a sad song sung by Shelley Fabares) while I watched out the window. The blue paper cover on the record (a 45-rpm) was exactly the same color as Mike's curtains!"

WHO HEARS THE FISH CRY?

NORMA FOX MAZER

STEALING-1

I'm shoplifting in Kersher's Music Store in the Northside Mall the day I meet Tyler Byrden for the first time. Northside Mall isn't really a mall, more a raggedy collection of stores scrunched together under one roof, and Kersher's isn't really a music store. It does sell some CDs and cassettes, but mostly coffee, donuts, ice cream, and candy. Maybe nothing is what it appears to be in Muntsville.

I'm pretending to be a browser while lifting an old Tina Tanniaka cassette and slipping it into a side pocket of my pants. Tina Tanniaka is a singer no one knows. She's totally berserk, and if I don't take the cassette, it will just languish here, which means *no one will hear her*. So in a way I'm doing a favor to music and to Tina Tanniaka, which is what I'm thinking when I look around and see this guy watching me.

Skinny blond guy. Nothing-special thin face coming down to a pointed chin. Vanilla ice cream guy. And he's staring at me. So I give him a stare—a glare stare, like I think he's a Mr. Macho hitting on me. As if. I swing past him, all haughty and innocent, like I don't know anything about anything, and walk right on out the door.

And he comes right on out after me.

MULTIPLE LIVES

"How many of you believe life and indeed all of human history is like a staircase that we keep climbing up?" Mr. Masichewski says the other day in AP history. And when nobody answers, he goes on, "I've just given you a common expression of a philosophical idea which has influenced plenty of big thinkers. So! Who wants to defend that idea? Who wants to knock it apart? Come on, freshmen, show me that you deserve to be in this class."

Janet Eckland raises her hand and everyone sort of shuffles and slinks down in their seats. Janet Eckland can talk. "I will defend that idea," she says, all perky. "I see my life like that. I mean, going upward. Rising. Higher and higher. It *is* like stairs!" She nods, agreeing with herself. "You keep going and then you get to the place where you want to be."

"And that is . . . ?" Mr. M. says.

"Well, wherever," Janet says, "but better than where you started."

"Ah. Why so?"

"Higher is better, Mr. M.," she says, and you can just hear the *duuuh* in her voice.

"Because . . . ?"

"Because you're older. You're independent. You do what you want. You get married and have sex and money."

Whistles. Clapping. Foot-stamping. Janet looks around and smiles.

"Whoa, people!" Mr. Masichewski says, and he calls on someone else.

Not me. I don't speak much in class—haven't since way

back in fourth grade. Sometimes I consider it, but then I figure, Why bother. If I did speak, though, on this particular subject, I would say that I know for a fact that if life is like a staircase, it's multiple. It's more than one set of stairs. You know how people always say we only have one life to live and we better make it count? That's a sneaky way of saying kids shouldn't do drugs or have sex, et cetera. But the point is, that only-one-life-to-live thing is not true.

I can testify to that. I've had Life One, I'm smack inside Life Two, and I gotta believe there's a Life Three coming up. I'm not Shirley MacLaine-ing here. Nothing so fancy. It's just this: Life One was my mom, my dad, and me. Marcy, Kevin, and Krystal. A regular American family. Until one day, either right before or right after my fourth birthday (Mom's not real clear on that detail), Kevin did the Big Walk-Out. You know. The he-went-to-the-store-for-a-pack-of-cigarettes-and-didn't-come-back-for-ten-years thing. Except ten years have been and gone, and he still hasn't come back with that pack of cigarettes.

My mom won't talk about it, but I think maybe Kevin got disgusted with her drinking. When I say this, though, she snorts, tosses her hair around, and says, "Who do you think taught me to love beer? You're off track, Krystal."

"Tell me the unsplit truth then, Mom, and put me back on track."

"The unsplit truth? Ma!" she calls to Grandma, who's wiping down the kitchen walls, a rag clutched in her knuckly hand. "Did you hear that, Ma?"

Grandma doesn't answer. She's not one for conversation. She has things to say and she says them, full decibel, when she's ready.

"So what's that mean—the unsplit truth?" Mom asks.

"The basic truth. The whole thing."

"Oh, uh-huh. Gotcha." Mom waves her cigarette in the air. "Well, maybe someday I'll tell you the whole thing. When I'm good and ready," she adds, giving me a Lady of Mystery look.

No mystery about Life Two. That began after Kevin left us, when Grandma moved in. She came with a suitcase and a bag of sugar cookies. She put the suitcase down in the hall and the cookies in the kitchen cupboard. Then she bent over, looked me in the eye, and said, "No cookies for you, my girl. Not now. Not until I know you're a good girl."

I was four years old. I knew I was a good girl. I dragged a chair over to the cupboard, climbed up on it, and reached for the cupboard door. I could almost taste that cookie in my mouth.

Grandma was quicker then and not so arthritic. She hauled me off the chair, plunked me down on the floor, and smacked me hard on the hand. "That hurts?" she said when I howled. "Good. I mean to bring you up right. I was too nice to your mama, and look at her. I'm not making that mistake again."

I know this is what she said, not because I was a four-year-old genius who remembered her every word but because I've heard those exact words so many times since then—those words and plenty more, not nearly so nice.

SHOVE

"Take me to the toilet." That's the first thing Grandma says every day when I come home from school and the reason I rush out the moment the bell rings. Grandma's spine is fused, her hands are swollen, and she has trouble doing certain things. Can't tie her shoes, can't button a dress, needs help in the bathroom—a whole list of stuff.

After the toilet I help her shower. After that it's, "Take out the garbage. . . ." "Vacuum the living room. . . ." "Put away the dishes. . . ." Then it's time to go to the grocery store. Grandma recites what we need: loaf of bread, quart of milk, five pounds of potatoes . . . whatever.

"You got that?" she asks.

"Yes."

She counts out money. "Bring me back the change. Don't think because I'm a helpless old woman you can take advantage of me. You hear me, Krystal?"

"Yes."

"You steal my money and you'll rot in hell."

I shove money and list into my pocket. I shove Grandma's voice into the box in my mind I've made for it and slam down the lid.

STEALING-2

I swing past Vanilla Boy, all haughty and innocent, like I don't know anything about anything, and walk right on out the door of Kersher's Music Store.

And he comes right on out after me.

"Are you following me?" I say, cold and hard.

"Hi," he says, like I just gave him a big hello, for God's sake! "I saw you take that."

"You saw me take what? What the hell are you talking about?"

I spit this out like I'm really really mad, not scared, not seeing myself hauled off to the police station in handcuffs, not already hearing Mom crying and Grandma screaming she always knew how I'd end up.

"Which one did you take?" Vanilla Boy says.

"I don't know what you're talking about."

"It was a cassette," he says.

"What are you, the store owner? An undercover cop?"

"I'm not going to turn you in," he says. "Who did you take? I think I know."

"If you know, why ask?" I stare at the pale lemon hair, the pale blue eyes, the acne on his chin. I pull the cassette out of my pocket. "You want it? Is that what this is all about? Here, take it."

"Tina Tanniaka," he says, looking but not taking. "I thought so. She's great."

Now I really stare, because this I don't believe. Nobody in Muntsville knows Tina Tanniaka except me. He must have been cheating. He must have been watching right over my shoulder. I put the cassette back in my pocket and I start to walk away.

"You didn't tell me your name," he calls.

"Well, *no kidding*," I say with great and obvious sarcasm.

He does not get it. He says, all solemn and good manners, "Tyler Byrden here."

A major geek! But then, probably because I'm grateful that he didn't rat me out, I say, "Krystal Cahill. Here," I add.

He sticks out his hand, and after a moment I put out mine, and we shake.

"*Crazy raisins,*" he says, which is a bizarre phrase from a Tina Tanniaka song.

I give him the only answer possible. "*Blazing blueberries.*" Which is from the same insane Tina Tanniaka song.

Then, even though I still don't believe that here is someone who actually knows Tina Tanniaka, I stand there a little longer, and we talk about her and her songs and we can't agree on anything. He says the greatest song she ever wrote is "Heart Like a Potato."

"No way! 'Move Over, Mountain Man,' " I say.

"No, no, no! Have you listened to 'Heart Like a Potato' recently?"

"Excuse me! Have you listened to 'Move Over, Mountain Man' lately?"

We get into it. We argue, he waves his arms around, and I try to shout him down. "You are fierce," he says, and his eyes are snapping. Pretty soon—I don't even notice how it happens—we're talking about a bunch of other stuff. And somewhere in there, I tell him how everything in the world appears weird, stupid, and awful to me but also hysterically funny.

"Even when no one else is laughing," he says.

"Especially when no one else is laughing."

And then we do this back-and-forth thing, almost like a routine, like we planned it or something, for God's sake.

He says, *"Weird when—"*

"—they tell you they love you—" I say.

"—'cause they want to feel better," he finishes.

Then I say, *"Stupid when—"*

"—they are so sure they know what you need—"

"—and what you are thinking."

And then together we say, *"Awful when—"*

And we talk over each other. He says, *"—when they sit at the table stuffing their faces so they don't have to talk to you."*

And I'm saying at the same time, *"—when they scream everything like they never learned to talk like normal people."*

"So what's funny?" he says.

"All of the above."

He scratches a pimple, makes a little bloody place. I give him a tissue and he sticks a scrap of it on the spot and asks, "So which was the first Tina Tanniaka song you ever heard?"

" 'Who Hears the Fish Cry?' "

"Same here," he says.

"The first one you ever heard?"

"Yup."

"You lie, you skinny mule!"

"I swear it's the truth. Boy Scout's honor." He raises three fingers.

"You were a Boy Scout?"

"A short career. They kicked me out."

"What for?"

"General weirdness."

Then it's really really corny, but we sing together, *"Who hears the fish when they cry? / Old Mr. Thoreau said it. / Baby, do you believe it? All those years ago! / I didn't know those folks back then were swift, / But when I saw that, it gave me such a crazy lift. / Fish cry, fish cry, fish crying in the water. / Why? Same reason you do, baby. Cruel, baby, cruel, / That's the world we're in. / Go on, lift up your chin, take a spin. / You may not win, but don't forget, / Old Mr. Thoreau, he said it all those years ago. / Who hears the fish when they cry cry cry cry cry cry CRY."*

And then we stand there some more and talk some more, and it's like we're twins who just got reunited, for God's sake.

BEING GOOD

In fourth grade my teacher, Mrs. Springer, had a pink face and hair that smelled like lemons. I wanted her for my own, and I went into practically full-time making up stories about her being my real mother, who'd had to give me away because she was poor but had been looking for me ever since, and once she knew the truth, we would be reunited forever and ever.

Oh, how I wanted Mrs. Springer to like me. Like me better than anyone. To *love* me. To love me more than anyone.

To earn that love, I talked.

I had noticed that all my teachers liked the kids who spoke up, the ones who raised their hands and knew the answers.

I began putting up my hand for every task and every question. I didn't wait for Mrs. Springer to call on me. I spoke up. *I will. . . . Let me. . . . The answer is, uh, the answer is . . . wait, wait, I'll get it. . . .*

"Krystal," she cried one day after I'd jumped up three times to offer the wrong answers, "don't you ever shut up?" Her pink face got pinker. "I'm sorry! I shouldn't have said that."

"Said what?" I asked.

"Shut up. That is not a nice way to talk."

"I don't care," I said, and I didn't. She could say shut up to me a hundred times, a thousand times, even a million times. It would still be just a little love tap to me compared to what Grandma said. "Mrs. Springer," I called.

"Yes, Krystal?" she sighed.

"Look." I clamped both hands over my mouth. Maybe I would never talk again. If that was what Mrs. Springer wanted, that was what I would do.

After that day I tried to be nicer and quieter, like other girls, but I wasn't good at it. Not good at all. I couldn't just sit still and quiet, because how would Mrs. Springer notice me if I did that? So I went on waving my hand in the air, springing up, and yelling out answers.

"You're a big problem," Mrs. Springer said one day. "What am I going to do with you, Krystal?"

Adopt me. Let me live with you. Be my mother.

She looked at me so intently, I knew she was reading my mind. I knew she was thinking about it. It was thrilling.

That same day she told our class we had been chosen to put on a play for the whole school. I could hardly believe my luck. I would take a part, I would be wonderful, and Mrs. Springer would love me so much that my whole life would be different. When she passed around the sign-up sheet, I signed my name twice.

"Stupid," the girl sitting next to me said.

I just smiled. This way I knew I would get a part.

Mrs. Springer kept me after school. She sat at her desk, her hands folded, and said, "Krystal, I'm taking your name off the sign-up sheet." She gave me that same intent look and said she was very sorry but I didn't know how to be part of a team. "I really can't have you in the play and use up all my energy trying to control you. Do you understand, Krystal?"

"Oh . . . yes!" I sang out. And I smiled, broad and big, the same way I smiled when Grandma told me that she knew from the moment she walked into the house all those years ago that I was bad news. And after that I did stop raising my hand and calling out answers, right or wrong.

In fifth grade I skipped school quite a few times. In sixth grade I skipped pretty regularly, and in seventh grade the truant officer came to our house. After he left, Grandma chased me around, whacking at me with her cane and crying out that everything she'd ever thought about me was true. "Sneak! Liar! You good-for-nothing. Trifling bit of dirt! Lousy kid! You'll never be any good."

BAG OF CHIPS

Every time I go into Quik Mart for chips or soda, I squint my eyes at the cashier, the pretty woman sitting on a high stool behind the counter, and I try to see her as if she's a stranger. The big dark hair cloud. The big flashy earrings. The big white smile. What do they add up to? Who is she? Then the line moves forward and I put my chips down on the counter and say, "Hi, Mom."

"Krys!" she says, like, Wow, what a surprise! She flashes me the smile everyone loves. "Hey, it's you! What're you doing here?"

I shrug and say, "Didn't see you last night, so . . ."

"Awww, honey. I got home late," she says, like it's a brand-new thing. "You were snoring away."

"You could wake me up. Where were you?" I play the game, say it like I don't know the answer.

"I was with my friends."

"Julie?"

She nods. Smiles. She likes that I know her friends.

"Mason?"

"Yeah. He's so cute!" She says this like she's sixteen. She leans over the counter. "Love you, my baby. Why do you always look so grim? Smile for Mama?"

Her face pushes close for a kiss, lips pouting out fat, sending me a whiff of minty breath. She sucks on those little red-and-white-striped candies all day.

"You coming home for supper?" I say.

"But of course."

Like she's there every night, regular as clockwork, and not hanging on a bar stool. And for about two seconds, I believe her.

I always do.

I take my chips and walk out, ripping the bag open and thinking how dumb I am. A really dumb person. Still believing something great is going to happen. Mom's going to change. Stop drinking. Start coming home at night.

You know those cartoon characters that get run over in the

road and lie there flat as a pancake, looking all dead? And then they sit up and rub their heads and go, "Oh, *duuh*, somethin' hit me." And they hop up, grinning and all happy, so stupid, so dumb they don't even know they're just going to get run over again.

CHANGE

In eighth grade I decided again to change myself. Be a new person. Someone good, someone sweet and nice. Someone Mrs. Springer would have liked. And in my mind, as soon as I decided to do it, it was a done deed. Like taking a shower and coming out all clean. Easy as that.

As if.

The thing is, I had a mouth. I had habits. Sometimes a temper. And try as I would, I kept blowing it. The intentions were good, but that wasn't enough. I went right on doing what I always did—mouthing off at anyone who got in my face, skipping school, stealing. I liked stealing. Didn't matter what it was—a pen, a book, money from Grandma's purse, a lipstick. Whatever. I liked the scary side of it, the daring side of it—thinking I'd be caught and then not being caught. And I liked having something that was someone else's—the secret of it. Sometimes I kept the stuff I took. Lots of times I gave it away. Once I was on a bus and a woman said, "What a pretty scarf," so I took it off and gave it to her. I liked doing that, too.

STEALING-3

Tyler Byrden and I stand out there on the sidewalk under the overhang of the Northside Mall, and we're talking like long-lost twins or something. We do not run out of things to talk about, and he does not act like he wants to get away, and I think, Is this real?

And then after a while I say, "Hang on, I'll be right back." And I go into Kersher's and put the Tina Tanniaka cassette back in the rack. I don't look out the window to see if Tyler's still there. If he's waiting for me. Or if he's gone now. I buy an ice cream cone. Vanilla, as a joke, which maybe I'll tell him about someday—like Mom says, When I'm ready.

I walk outside, licking the ice cream, and he's not there.

Riiight. Big stupid surprise.

I lick the cold ice cream, and I'm laughing inside at how dumb I am. I put the cassette back for him. Trying to impress him. So how much have I learned since Mrs. Springer and fourth grade?

I throw the cone down on the sidewalk and mash it all around with my sneaker.

"Why are you doing that?" a voice says in my ear.

I turn. "Mr. Vanilla himself!"

He blinks a little. "What?"

"Never mind! Never mind! Where were you?"

I hear myself sounding like Grandma. Screaming, scared and mean. I don't know what to do. I could smash my head against a wall. Or throw myself in front of a car. I walk away. I come back. I twirl around in a circle. I'm crazy. Crazy as my grandma.

"*Stay clam and nobody will get hurt,*" he says. Which is another insane Tina Tanniaka line.

And that is so good, so perfect. *Stay clam and nobody will get hurt.* I want to say something. I want to say *crazy raisins* or *blazing blueberries.* Something. Anything. But I can't. I can't speak. I just stand there and stare at him.

"I saw what you did," he says.

Isn't that what he said when I came out with the cassette? Which was—it now seems—at least a week ago. A month ago. Another life ago.

"In the store," he says. "I was watching you. You put it back."

"Oh . . . *that,*" I get out. And I shrug, like it's the merest nothing, a trifle, a tiny gesture that I hardly knew I made.

"They didn't see you," he says.

I nod.

"They didn't see you take it, and they didn't see you put it back."

I nod again.

"Mondo weirdo," he says.

"Insane," I agree.

And we sit down on the sidewalk, our backs against a wall, and we go on talking like we never stopped.

CRAZY

"Jeez Louise," Mom said one day when Grandma had been louder and meaner than usual, "that woman has been traveling on the road to crazy for years, and it sounds like she's just about got there."

"That woman is your mother," I said.

"Well, thank you for the information, Krystal."

"Was she always crazy like this?"

"Was she always— Let me think about that. . . . Well, maybe not as bad as she is now. But, yeah, she was probably always a terrible woman."

"You say she's terrible, but we live with her. How come we just live with her and don't do anything about it?"

Mom shrugged. "What do you want me to do? I can't kick her out in the street. She's here. We're stuck. Anyway, it's not so bad if you're careful."

"It's bad," I said, "and you know it. You got away from her once," I added.

"Uh-huh. Your dad came along, and that was it for me. Such a good-looking guy. No dummy, either," she said, and smiled her pretty smile, as if Kevin's coming along had been a really good thing all around.

Okay, I guess it wasn't a *total* bad thing. I mean, I'm here— for whatever that's worth. But the fact is, Mom didn't know what she was doing when she went with Kevin—she just did it. She didn't know what she was doing when she told Grandma to come live with us. Mom never had a plan. She was always a going-along person, and she's still a going-along person. She works, she does the bar scene, and she hands over her life and her money to whoever is there ready to take it.

What's she going to do when I leave? Because I am going to leave. That's one thing I know for sure. Everything else is just all questions and no answers. But on that one point, I'm positive. As soon as I graduate, I'm out of here. I'm gone. I'll go as fast and as far as Greyhound will take me. *I've* got a plan. It's simple. It's called the Whatever-You-Do-Don't-Do-What-Mom-Did Plan.

THE DRY SMELL OF GLADNESS

There was this one day when Grandma was screaming at me, telling me I was no good and going to hell and all that sort of thing. No different from a hundred other times, but for some reason I just couldn't stand it that day.

"Yeah, Grandma," I said. "You're right, I'm going someplace. I'm going there right now." And I walked out of the house.

She screamed after me to come back, that I had work to do, that I was rotten and bad.

I walked away and I kept walking, thinking that maybe I was on my way to Greyhound and a real somewhere else a whole lot sooner than I'd planned.

I kept walking. Muntsville is not so big that you can get lost, but I managed to do it. I walked myself right out of Muntsville, and then I kept walking, and I walked until I dead-ended on a dirt road surrounded by weedy fields, with not a house, a horse, a person, or even a dog anywhere in sight.

I was tired and maybe crying a little. I do that sometimes when no one is around. I stopped and leaned against a tree and looked up at the sky, and I hated how blue it was. How perfect.

Then the weirdest thing happened. The sky looked back at me.

It looked back at me, and it was quiet and blue and just *there*, like it loved me or something.

And then the same strange thing happened with the trees and the weeds and the dirt road. They were all looking at me, I swear they were, peaceful and calm, like they were telling me something and waiting for me to get it.

And I did. I got it.

I got that the trees and the sky and the road and even the weeds in the field—they didn't care if I was happy or unhappy, if I was sad or mad, good or bad. They just went on being what they were. Weeds. Trees. Sky. And that was enough. That was all they had to be.

And then I was like that too. . . . Not good or bad, not wanting anything. Just there. And I was all calm and full of something . . . like peace, or maybe it was what they call happiness.

It was like sun heat or water, like a river of cool water, sliding and gliding through me.

I sat down, and then I lay down and stretched out my arms and looked up at the sky. And for a few moments that was all I wanted, the dry and dusty scent of the road and the blue sky over me.

STEALING-4

After a while Tyler and I are sitting on the sidewalk, our backs against a wall, and we're talking like we'll never stop. Then Tyler, all of a sudden he sort of ducks his head, and he doesn't even look like Vanilla Boy anymore, and he says, "Krystal."

He says my name, like that. "Krystal."

And I say, "Tyler." And I like saying it. So I say it again. "Tyler." I touch his lips. I don't know why, I just want to, so I do.

And he says, "You want to kiss?"

"I don't care," I say. "It's okay, if you want to."

But when our faces get close together, I almost can't breathe. He smells like bread or something, maybe pinecones, just something very good.

Our lips touch, and it's different, it's so different, it's not like anything I ever knew or felt or thought . . . or knew I wanted.

It's . . . it's the blue sky again, and the weeds and the trees and the road.

"Oh. Wow," I mumble against his lips, which I know you're not supposed to do when you kiss. But except for Jimmy Monroe, who threw me in the snow and pushed his dirty face against mine back in fourth grade, no boy has ever kissed me. So I don't have any practice doing it right.

I don't want to ever stop.

We don't.

We sit there, kissing and kissing and kissing.

"You kids!" someone says, walking past us, and we still don't stop.

We kiss and kiss and kiss.

And his face is all shiny and red when we finally break apart, and probably mine is too. And then he does something even more wonderful. He leans toward me again and he licks my lips and then he licks my eyelids.

"Okay," I gasp, and I stagger to my feet, gripped by something both sweet and terrible, knowing I will never be the same again.

About Norma Fox Mazer

Norma Fox Mazer is the author of many novels for young adults, including *Taking Terri Mueller; Silver; Heartbeat* (cowritten with her husband, Harry Mazer); *When She Was Good; Good Night, Maman;* and *Girlhearts.* Her novel *A Figure of Speech* was a National Book Award nominee; *After the Rain* was named a Newbery Honor Book, a *Horn Book* Fanfare, an ALA Notable Children's Book, and, along with many of her other books, an ALA Best Book for Young Adults. Norma has edited acclaimed collections of both stories and poetry, including *Dear Bill, Remember Me?,* and has been honored with the Christopher Award, the Edgar Allan Poe Award for Best Juvenile Mystery, and two Lewis Carroll Shelf Awards. She is on the faculty of the Vermont College Master of Fine Arts in Writing for Children and Young Adults program.

Norma writes, "There was a boy in high school whom I found *very* desirable and *very* unavailable (not interested, big man on campus, squiring prom queen, *waaaay* out of my earnest, high school journalist, A-student, uncool league), and then came a moment when we were face to face—or more accurately, knee to knee—in a girlfriend's motorboat, and I turned on the BigSmile, the VeryBiiigSmile . . . and he leaned forward, smiling, my heart going pit-a-pat just like they said in stories, wondering, Is it possible, could he be falling for me? Me? Closer, closer he came, face almost touching mine and then, leaning back, as if satisfied, he said, 'Wow! You have really big front teeth!' So maybe I wrote this story to give that kiss I never got to Krystal—who really needed it."

DRIVING HER WILD

JENNIFER ARMSTRONG

THE FIRST time was supposed to be special. Not everyone understood that, but Cheryl did. Some people just went ahead and did it randomly, without forethought. Just. Like. That. Ask them afterward what it was like and all they could say was, "Great. It was awesome," with a dazed look in their eyes. "Kinda scary, but cool." Too many kids were just that casual about it. But by the time Cheryl was sixteen, she had planned every detail about how it would be for her, right down to what she would wear and what music to have on.

She had been planning it, revising it, changing and refining the details of her plan since she was thirteen, since she first realized that of course there would be a *first* time, and she wanted to be able to remember every detail when it actually happened. Because it changed people. Cheryl understood that. It was obvious, really. The kids who had already done it—they held themselves differently, like they knew other people were looking at them and enjoyed having people look at them. A way of holding their heads, a kind of breathless laugh in the hallway between classes. They even seemed to move in slow motion, like people moving through water, forcing ripples out ahead of themselves and behind themselves and on all sides as they moved. It was what separated kids from grown-ups. There were the ones who hadn't done it—the babies, the children, the pathetic losers—and then there were the ones who had: Them.

When Cheryl's sixteenth birthday had finally arrived, her best friend, Amanda, put a Sweet Sixteen banner up across her locker and made a point of telling everyone it was Cheryl's birthday. All day long boys would stop Cheryl in the hall outside the auditorium or on the way to the media center and sing that goofy song, belting it out while they sank to one knee: *"Girrrrl! You'll be a womaaaaan soooon. Sooooon, you'll need a man."*

And that evening her parents, after the presents and the cake and all, had sat her down for the Talk, Cheryl's mother saying, "We just want to be sure you understand the consequences—" and Cheryl interrupting, "I know all about it," so patiently, so maturely. "We've been talking about it in health and safety class since seventh grade. About being responsible, knowing your limits."

Cheryl's dad had clearly been a little uncomfortable, rubbing his palms across his knees, probably thinking his little girl was suddenly becoming a woman—frightening, really—and saying with a blush, "If you're ever at a party and some boy gives you some alcohol to drink, and I'm not saying we expect you to be Little Miss Prissy," he rushed on, his voice rising as if he was trying to convince himself, "but if you find yourself in over your head, you can call us. No matter what time it is. You don't have to be embarrassed. We won't be mad at you."

So of course Cheryl had been a little indignant, saying, "I'm not going to get drunk and do something stupid, Dad. You know me better than that."

There probably weren't any parents in the world who thought the typical teenager was old enough, but if they were honest with themselves, they'd have to admit that they all did it as soon as they could, some of them probably even younger than sixteen. The ones who grew up in the country, for example. But Cheryl wasn't really upset with her parents. It was to be expected.

Because it was big. It was a big thing. Sometimes in the middle of the day—in physics class, maybe, or standing in line for lunch—Cheryl would look around and wonder how many kids were thinking about it at that exact moment. To be honest, she thought about it almost all the time, desperate to grow up. At the end of school sometimes she'd see twelfth graders leaving the parking lot, driving away in their cars, so cool, and she would just be *aching* for it, standing there feeling like a puny little infant but feeling so ready for it in every single atom of her being. Standing there waiting for her bus and feeling that a mistake had been made somewhere.

One day Cheryl was sitting with Amanda in the cafeteria and some boys at the table behind them were talking about it, this one guy talking about his first time, how far he went and how fast, and for how long, with *sound* effects even. Cheryl felt her back prickling with the intensity of listening in, and she knew Amanda was listening too. They caught each other's glance and Amanda rolled her eyes as if to say, "Boys, they're obsessed," but Cheryl knew her friend wanted it as much as she did. Suddenly Cheryl realized her mouth was open, she was breathing through her mouth, and her cheeks felt flushed, and her lips were so dry she wanted to lick them—but then she felt so horrifyingly self-conscious, as though everyone would know what she had been thinking about, that she just ducked her head over her copy of *Silas Marner* and reached for her soda with a fumbling hand. If people only knew what was going through my mind, she thought, amazed that it wasn't flashing in neon over her head. The door shuts. Finally, you're alone. . . .

Her fantasy was remarkably elaborate, but not that remarkable, perhaps, given how much time she spent polishing it. Some kids would rush into it, so totally psyched they wouldn't be able to see straight, but Cheryl wanted it to be slower than that, more deliberate. The current version of the fantasy involved going home after school, maybe having a bite to eat and watching a little TV, then so calmly, so nonchalantly, standing up, stretching—it's time. She knew how it would be, the turning, the hesitation and the yielding, the stopping, and then going on, going faster, this rush, this intoxication of finally, *finally* driving the car on her own, free, the chains of childhood spinning off at last into the ditch at the side of the road.

She couldn't wait.

ABOUT JENNIFER ARMSTRONG

Jennifer Armstrong has written over fifty books for children and teenagers, including *The Dreams of Mairhe Mehan; Shipwreck at the Bottom of the World; In My Hands: Memories of a Holocaust Rescuer;* and *Chin Yu Min and the Ginger Cat.* You can read more about her award-winning titles at www.jennifer-armstrong.com. She lives in Saratoga Springs, New York, where she is always at work on another book.

She writes, "What I remember most about being a teenager was wanting so many things—to be older, to be smarter, to be prettier, to be somewhere else, to have my own car, to be the object of desire, to be admired, to be famous, to make my mark. Desire often made me miserable, but it drove me ever onward."

THE COUNTY FAIR

VICTOR MARTINEZ

EVERY YEAR, as the days shrink and trees turn ashen and leaves sail like yellow boats through the boulevards, the newspapers in my town stamp bolder and bolder headlines about the county fair. This year they splashed photos of the Cotton Queen, with a long white dress and sparkling diamond crown, waving her little porcelain hand at me.

Usually I don't like crowds, at downtown shopping malls or wherever people press and plow about, but the crowds at the fair start my brain whirling, and I can almost surrender my own heartbeat to the countless hearts beating around me. Some years I even biked over to the fairgrounds to watch the huge semis and Peterbilt trucks roll in, their brakes hissing and trailers shunting as they dipped through the gated entrance. They'd unload farm animals, lash and hoot them into their tiny corrals. They'd forklift crates of Thompson grapes, peaches, oranges, apples, walnuts, everything grown in the valley where I lived.

Most exciting, though, was watching the workmen crank up the rides: bumper cars, the Hammer, the Octopus, the Ferris wheel and Half-apples. Nothing put me on needles more than the thought of veering madly in the Half-apples, ribbons of saliva slinging from my mouth, or being tossed in the revolving baskets, where just by turning a wheel you could spin as fast as you dared. To be dumped on the walk plank, swooning and breathless—that was my kind of happiness!

This year I knew it was going to be better. This year I made a date with Carol Maldonado, one of the girls who photographed the smiles for the school yearbook and who was headed to college with neat tepees of A's on her report card. She who was standing in front of me in the lunch line of the high school cafeteria. At first I couldn't choke up a word. You could have tapped my throat and heard a hollow echo, I was so scared. I was fumes, that's all, fumes and vapors, and I hardly felt my hand touch the spoon and fork in the cradle of utensils. But then, I don't know how, I staunched my fear and asked her.

She was wearing bell-bottom jeans with a scarf tied through the belt loops, and she had my friend Pete's two-toned letter jacket on. He won it for wrestling and gave it to her on a whim, although he wasn't her boyfriend. Summer still shone healthy on her face, and she wore a ponytail, which she whipped around whenever she turned, like she did when she turned toward me.

"What's your name?"

"Roybal," I said, disappointed that she didn't know.

"Roy, huh." She thought for a long minute. "Okay, Roy, do you have a car?"

"No, but I could borrow one." My dad, who was a janitor, doesn't work on Wednesday nights, and I figured his panel truck, with excuses, would do in a pinch.

"What about money, do you have any money?"

"Sure, I got lots of money." I patted my pocket, but she knew it was dry. How could I have money when I didn't own a car? Lately the bills stuffing our mailbox had Mom squeezing her fist tight to shut off the flow of happiness through our house. For weeks, she'd been feeding us misery meals of corn tortillas, beans and rice, the same potato tacos day after day. Knowing I couldn't beg one measly buck from her, I got work lifting onion sacks into a sorting machine, gave her half the money, and stashed the rest for the fair.

Carol thought long over my proposal. We were walking out of the lunch line when she finally said, "Okay, Roy, when do you want to go?"

"Wednesday."

The next thing I needed was to borrow my dad's truck. I began to seriously whittle at his stubbornness one night while he watched TV, but he just chomped on his toothpick and shook his head. When I told him it was for a girl, he spit the toothpick out and grinned in amazement. Me, with a girl? Me, who blushed red whenever Sarah came from next door to borrow sugar? The thought of it tickled him but sort of made him proud too, like I'd passed a test in his eyes. So he lent me the truck, even managed with his generous right hand to pry from the stingy fingers of his left hand a few dollars to buy Carol some cotton candy, or better yet, he suggested eagerly, a gummy-headed caramel apple.

Carol's house was on a quiet street; not like ours, crowded with traffic that foamed noise inside your ear all day. Our house had a porch that winced and a roof overhang that drooped like a lazy eye; hers had a mailbox stall and a lawn buzzed clean by regular mowing. When I drove up her gravel driveway, a flinty suspicion sparked across her mom's eyes when she saw how rusty my dad's old panel truck was. She leaned her hand on the hood, surveying the spectacle. The front tire was half dead. There were no side-view mirrors, and the engine sounded close to losing a gut just idling there. I had to bang on the frozen door handle about five times before it worked. I thought for sure she'd call the date off, but she had that sloshed look that drink causes when it frees the muscles on a face.

She let Carol get in, but not before making a motherly show of adjusting the seat so Carol could sit nice and proper. Then she stretched the door all the way to the hinge and to my surprise let in Carol's little sister, Susie, who gave me a couple sissy pushes before scrunching between us. She leaned forward, excited, and put her tiny hands on the dashboard. That's when Carol caught the lingering smell of rotting melons and covered her nose.

"Oh yeah," I said, "my dad got them from a farmer's field. They'd just rot anyway. Some of them were rotten when he picked them. That's why it still smells."

"He probably stole them," Carol said, arching her back.

"No, he didn't steal them," I said, bruised by her thinking my dad was a thief.

She eyed me like she knew I was sensitive but stupid, then smiled halfway. "Oh, whatever," she said, pressing her finger against her neck as if to search for a pulse. "I hate that smell, though."

I sat back and pinched my eyebrows together. I was going to ask her why she hated the smell of melons when I caught Carol's mom sneaking over to the rear window to peek inside. I think she was checking to see if any strange boys were hiding there.

"Roy, you make sure you get her back early," she said, coming around.

"I will, don't worry, Mrs. Maldonado." I tried my best to sound mature.

Carol's mom was shaking her head, and her eyes had serious fishhooks when we pulled away. I smiled and waved a slack hand at her. She said, "Carol, you stay with Susie. Don't let her out of your sight."

"I will, Mama," Carol said tiredly, like she'd sung this song a hundred times before.

About a block from the fair, cars with curlicues of light jiggling across their windshields and dappling along the side doors moved bumper to bumper along the street. Carol kept leaning across my knees, flirting with some guys she knew in a car edging ours. They had their own girlfriends, though, with makeup thick as the icing on birthday cakes, and they giggled like cold water was splashing on their necks. Carol was prettier than any of them any day. She wore a dress with a blue and cream cardigan, and she didn't have her hair tied in a ponytail anymore but fluffed over her shoulders. Once, when her soft stomach pressed against my knees, I could feel this sludge of warm oil gurgling inside my chest. She looked up at my face, which must have had a stony stare, because she teased, "Night of the Living Dead!"

From a distance we could see the double Ferris wheel reeling, its red and orange sidelights smearing the blackened sky. We could see the Hammer ride swinging as if to pound on the ground, then rising up again. I saw this man in a suit escorting this gorgeous lady in a silky dress that shimmered when she moved. I dreamed for a second: If only that was Carol and me. Everybody in school would nose around us like jealous fish.

We found a parking space on a curb after about twenty minutes of circling. An old man dressed in overalls with a boiling crown of white hair came over from his porch, where he'd been watching a TV Western. Massaging his wrist like he was wearing a watch, he said the space was his and he charged a dollar and fifty cents to park there. I started to climb back in the truck when Carol fingered a dollar and two quarters from her purse and pushed them into the man's hand.

"I hope you take care of the car," she said.

"Don't worry, missy, I take care of all the cars on my lot, even yours." He kicked off a cake of mud stuck on the tire treads. Then he chuckled and hunched over his porch to watch guns going off and horses thundering across a desert on the TV.

As soon as we pushed through the entrance chute, Carol, swiping back her hair, walked quickly away. When I caught up to her, she said that what she really wanted to do was to meet with her friend Mina and listen to rock-and-roll bands at the stadium.

"Hey!" I said as she walked away. "What about Susie?"

Carol slowed down to think this over. "Keep an eye on her."

"I thought you were going to stay with me?"

"Well, I can't. I have commitments."

She started to walk away again, so I said—and this was all I could think of—"Your mom will kill you if she finds out you left Susie alone with me."

"Hey, wait a minute. You never said I had to stay with you." Then, she looked at me, cautious, like she was hiding behind her face all of what she didn't dare say. Suddenly, from the corner of her eye, she spied Susie dashing off. I saw her too and searched Carol's face. She gave me a hopeless, exasperated look and rushed after her.

Susie plopped her tiny arms on a game-booth counter to watch a man with butch-cut hair and a flashy green Hawaiian shirt toss plastic rings at rows of standing bottles. He'd throw the rings into the air in high, floating arcs, hoping to loop them around the bottlenecks. Most pinged off the glass tops, but he'd already won a two-foot pink dog with fluffy, cotton-candy fur and floppy black ears. He wanted to ring enough to exchange the dog for a giant panda and was already shoving his beefy fingers into his wallet.

Taking her chin off the counter, Susie ran over to me, bouncing and begging for money. Carol stayed at the booth, a hand on her hip.

"Well," I said when I walked over, "maybe we could just hang around together. Maybe we could take care of Susie together."

Carol shook her chin slowly, sizing me up, then adjusted the shoulder of her cardigan, like already the night was getting too long. "Maybe for a while," she said.

Just then a puff of wind brought in the smell of damp wood and ripened fruit. It came from a nearby building that housed the fruits and vegetables for the agricultural fair. Although they were only supposed to be for admiring, being a little hungry, I thought of stealing some nibbles from the grape and cherry displays.

"I don't want to go in there," Carol said, guessing my thoughts. "It stinks!"

"No, no," I assured her. "That's the livestock fair."

"No, that's the place I mean, the agricultural fair. It smells like rotting melons."

"It doesn't smell like rotting melons," I said. "My dad's truck smells like rotting melons."

"Well, it smells like work, anyway. It smells like work!" she insisted, dropping her hand. She stared into my face a moment and turned away.

I got to thinking then about what she meant by hating the smell of melons. Before my dad got the janitor job, for as long as I remember, we—my mother, father, my younger brother, Caleb, and I—worked in the fields. Considering how Carol acted at school, like she was insulted over not living in a mansion, or like she was only waiting for her *real* parents to come in a limousine to claim her, I figured that's what the smell reminded her of, picking crops, which maybe her family did once, I didn't know.

That's when Susie began pulling on my pants pocket, like kids do when they suspect licorice is inside. She wanted to ride the baby cars. "Sure, honey," I said, bending down to tie her shoelace. As I did, I started imagining being Susie's father, and Carol my wife. She wouldn't like being married to me, though, that's for sure. I'd never have enough money for her, and I'd never really be anybody enough to earn her respect. I got disgusted with myself for thinking that way, but that was the truth of it. School, jobs, what the teachers said about my grades, what the counselor advised me about my college prospects—I could see it all too clearly.

We had to walk a ways, but Susie got to ride on the tiny cars that dipped as they went around and around. Carol waved at her as she passed, and I watched a guy in a game booth pitch softballs at a triangle of lead bottles.

After Susie got her thrills, I coaxed her into riding the Octopus with me by telling her it was just as scary as the baby cars. To my surprise, she jumped up and down, excited, and when we got to the ticket booth, she walked bravely to the height line. She had to tiptoe to reach it, but luckily the ticket lady turned her head to pop fresh gum into her mouth. Susie was bouncing on the seat, clapping her hands and screeching, when suddenly, with a loud crank, our heads lurched and we were hurled into the dizzying night.

It took about a second to figure out why they had the height line in the first place. Susie's tiny body didn't really fit snug inside the clamping bar, so after about the third pass she slipped to the floor. There she began worming around, making whining noises. Afraid that she'd fly out through an opening at the bottom, I was relieved when she planted her cheek against my knee and she took a death grip on my leg.

After the ride we couldn't stop her bawling. I gave her a quarter and Carol stroked her hair, saying, "Baby, baby." I even gave her a phony speech about how brave she was just for trying that ride. She threw the quarter in my face. Planting her knuckles in her watery eyes, Susie blubbered something about telling her mom, so I rushed over to a stand and bought her a corn dog, smearing on globs of mustard. Finally she quieted down, holding the corn dog and twisting her fist against her runny nose, making little squeaky noises. "I'm still gonna tell Mom," she muttered.

That's when Carol and I looked at each other and laughed.

That was a good laugh. It showed we were together for once. Susie would have nothing to do with more rides, though, and Carol didn't seem too excited either, especially after seeing the long tails of waiting lines. We did stop at a basketball-game booth, though. Three balls for a dollar, so I asked Carol if I could try it.

"Hey, I'm not your boss," she said, but she came over to watch.

The tiny hoops hardly let the skin of the balls pass through, and when my first two shots hit the rim, they splattered like water off a hot greasy pan. On my last ball I got lucky, and the guy with the dirty apron and big pockets gave me another ball for free. When I banked that one in with a *thunk*, he wedged a foam lizard under my arm, flattering me on how it was too easy for a dead-eye shooter like me to swish those tiny balls into those big wide hoops.

"Wait a minute," I said, warming over my triumph. I was dreaming hard about winning a larger pink dog, then giving it over with a flourish to Carol. The guy winked and made out like I was taking advantage of him, like maybe next I'd ask for his car keys. This was all an act, of course. He probably figured I was lucky to get the first two balls in, so when I fished out another dollar, he did a fancy bow and served me the ball on the tray of his hand. This time I sank all three in a row. Two barely pinged the rim, and the other smacked off the backboard and ripped through the net.

I was pointing at one of the pink dogs hanging along the booth, when the guy, seeing how easy I sank the baskets, said, "Hey, what the hell is this? You're leaning too much over the counter."

"What?" I said, surprised at how quick his voice turned edgy.

"No, no, you can't lean over the counter like that!"

"I wasn't leaning over the counter."

"Yeah you were! Hey, what kind of trick you pulling here, anyway?"

"I'm not pulling any trick," I said.

"Yeah," Carol said coming over. "He made them fair and square."

"Watch your mouth, girlie," the guy said, making a stop sign with his hand. Then he scrambled over to the side to pick up balls.

I was still trying to figure out why he was so nice one minute, mean the next, when Carol asked this young guy whose girlfriend had her head cradled on his shoulder if he saw anything sneaky. The guy raised his hand, not wanting to get involved. When his girlfriend, with blond hair combed straight and split down the middle, pinched him on the belly, he lifted his arm again and said firmly, "I *told* you, I didn't see anything."

When Carol started searching the crowd for other witnesses, they scattered like somebody had just thrown a firecracker at their feet. That's when the booth man came over and threw me another foam lizard.

"Here you go, chief," he said, then moved away to the other end of the booth. I knew then it was hopeless to argue.

"Come on, let's get out of here," I told Carol.

"Wait a minute," she protested, pulling on my arm. "That guy cheated you."

"I know. I know, but there's nothing we could do about it," I said, handing the lizards to Susie, who started play-fighting with them.

By then the booth man was hollering in his loud voice for more shooters. He pretended to be busy with some guys in letter jackets who came over, daring each other to give it a try.

"Here we go," the man said. "Some real honest-to-God basketball players."

I didn't want to start a commotion, but Carol, well, I could hear her hissing between her teeth. Then some biker guys with dust-shiny jeans and decaled jackets came out of nowhere and told us to get the hell out of their way, so I grabbed Carol by the arm.

"Hey, maybe we should leave," I told her. "It's getting late."

Carol just looked at me strange, lifting her upper lip away from her teeth and grinning. When she saw how I kept turning warily around, expecting one of those bikers to come and grab me by the shoulder, she shook her head in disgust.

"How long," she said, slow and easy, like she was squeezing out each word, "how long are you going to let those people push you around? They don't do it to other people. They only do it to us. The guy at the parking lot, that guy there, and those guys with their stupid jackets—they think they can say and do anything they want to us."

"Carol, look, I'm not about to go fighting everybody who . . ." That's when I stopped. I stopped because I knew she was right, and I had no answer. Thinking about it made it hurt, but talking about it made it worse because there was nothing to do about it. That's when I yelled to a man passing by in a tan blazer, "Hey, mister! Do you know what time it is?"

The man looked at his watch, a big square one with glowing numbers, and said, "It's nine o'clock."

"Come on, let's get out of here. It's getting late." I waved, trying to hurry her along. Carol must have known I wasn't serious because she just stood there, pumped with anger, not moving, her face an icy moon. Finally she couldn't stand it any longer and started to say something, but then, whatever her words were, whatever she thought about what had happened or about me suddenly went out of her face, like it wasn't really important. Instead, she slowly turned her shoulder and walked away, not even bothering to worry about Susie.

Dragging Susie along with me, I was feeling pretty frustrated about the game-booth guy when I caught up with Carol. I just couldn't figure out why he'd risk turning away customers by being so cheap with a lousy pink dog. "Where're you going?" I asked her.

"I just want to listen to the music," she said, walking faster, and swerving through the crowds of people.

Letting go of Susie but keeping an eye on her, I tagged alongside Carol.

"Well, we aren't gonna make it home by nine-thirty, you know," I said, like suddenly I was a stickler for time. She stopped and glared at me again.

"Where? Where do you have to go so all of a sudden, Roybal? What do you have to do? What's so important in your life that you have to be there right on time?"

"I'm supposed to take you home."

"Why? Why do you have to take me home? What am I going to do there? Watch my mother sleep on the couch?"

I'm a patient guy, usually. I can fiddle with a hangnail for an hour, or watch tree branches wave in the wind, but suddenly what she said made me feel impatient, like everything was running away from me and I had to catch up to it fast or I'd lose it forever. That's when I noticed Susie squirming beside me, pinching her legs together. She had to go pee. "Okay, let's go!" I huffed, steering her shoulders to the rest room. I waited for her, and when she came back out, I held her by the hand, searching for Carol.

She was gone. Looking over people's heads, I couldn't see her, but then Susie spotted her in a herd of people filing in through the chain-link fence at the stadium. Once inside, I saw her and her friend Mina talking to some guys near the stage. Susie broke from my hand and rushed down the stadium aisle, refusing to turn when I called her back. I watched her tiny head bob in and out of the clusters of people in the aisles. I yelled to her to tell Carol let's go.

"I want to leave right now," I shouted. "Not later! Right now!" But I knew she was too small to listen.

Making my own way down the aisle, I came across Mina, who had her hair teased tough and wore a skirt tight around her hips. She had a monkey bite ripe as a plum on her neck, and glossy lipstick. She was with a Mexican guy, bone-skinny, wearing cowboy boots and a tilted Texas hat. Carol, to my surprise, was sitting with this older guy dressed in a gray marines uniform. Studs and little boxes of colored puzzles hung on his chest, and he wore a round, flat hat with a gold eagle on the visor. I couldn't see his pants, but I knew they had a red stripe down the sides, which my dad once told me represented the blood of Mexicans killed in the war between the United

States and Mexico. He sat straight while Carol lay crushed against him, her arm clutching his, her eyes looking everywhere but at me.

The group of mariachis that came on after the rock bands began winding into the first song, and the people behind hollered at me to sit down and for the marine and Mina's boyfriend to take off their hats. The marine-guy did it right away, patting his neat hair, but Mina's boyfriend stood up and in raunchy Spanish told the people to calm down their complaining farts. He took off his hat, though. There wasn't a seat for me, so I sat in the aisle, still trying to catch Carol's eye and wondering what I'd do if she did look at me. The mariachis, about eight of them, decked out in black with straps and spangles and studs, sang *"La Negra"* and *"México, Lindo y Querido."* And with that one, I noticed Carol's face turn mushy with emotion. Mina's boyfriend let out a Mexican *grito* so loud it echoed across the stadium.

I didn't get mad when the marine-guy, holding Carol's hand, walked us back to the truck. And I didn't get embarrassed when every once in a while he'd pat my shoulder like I was his buddy. Listening to the mariachis had calmed me down and I said to no one in particular that my dad, who I knew was right then waiting for me, might like that they had mariachis at the fair.

When we got to the truck, Carol and the guy gave each other about a hundred kisses good-bye. He fiddled romantically with a button on her cardigan, then swept his hand across her neck before leaving. I helped Carol into the front seat and lifted Susie onto her lap. Susie was kissing the foam lizards' snouts together, mimicking Carol and her boyfriend's endless good-bye. I cranked up the engine and *vroomed* the gas pedal. At the first red light, I saw the Hammer coming up and down with people screaming in fright.

All the way home, I couldn't stop thinking about everything that had happened and what Carol had said to me, trying to find something in it that would explain why my chest felt crumpled like a bad test paper. There was a strange sadness in me that I didn't understand and I sensed I never would. About the marine, there was no mistaking—it was him Carol liked, and it was him she really wanted to be with at the fair. She probably figured her mother would think him too old for her. Fingering her hair and staring listlessly out the window at the houses drifting past, she was quiet all the way home.

When I drove up her driveway, before I jumped out to open her door, Carol touched me on the arm like there was no need for me to keep being polite. She still didn't look at my eyes, though, only glanced at my shoulder and then the dashboard. I told Susie she could keep the lizards, but she paid me no mind as she played at making them talk.

Over the steering wheel I watched Carol walk up the front steps and put the key in the door, the porch light haloing her hair, still ruffled from her boyfriend's hand. She didn't turn around, didn't wave good-bye or anything. Her back told me clearly that I was someone far away. I don't know why, but suddenly, at that moment, I felt like something inside me was being squeezed out. I knew that whatever it was would soon be gone forever, but all I could think of was my dad, at home, waiting eagerly for me to tell him about my date.

ABOUT VICTOR MARTINEZ

Victor Martinez is the author of *Parrot in the Oven: Mi Vida*, a National Book Award winner, a *Horn Book* Fanfare Honor Book, and a *Publishers Weekly* Best Book of the Year. Mr. Martinez has also published a collection of poems called *Caring for a House*. He presently lives in San Francisco's Mission District.

LOVING MEGAN

NANCY GARDEN

"THERE SHE is," I whispered to Kat, sliding my lunch tray along the table so I'd be next to her. "There's Megan."

Katherine Emily Rogers, who'd been my best friend forever, looked up skeptically from her tuna salad. Then she looked again, her brown puppy-dog eyes wide with what I could only interpret as heartfelt wonder.

"See?" I said. "See what I mean?"

Kat nodded silently. Then she murmured, "Yes, Penny, I do. Oh, yes!"

Megan, the object of my—and I thought *our*—admiration, was a senior, and we were freshmen. She was captain of the cross-country team and president of the drama club; I'd managed to find that much out in the first week of school. And she was gorgeous. Drop-dead, perfect, stunning, magnificent gorgeous.

Her corn-silk blond hair fell into a thick mane, held at the nape of her neck with either a scrunchy or a black velvet ribbon, depending, I decided, on whether she felt playful or sophisticated that day. We'd already noticed—I had, anyway— that she always wore the same long blue-and-yellow silk scarf, sometimes wrapped casually around her neck and draped over one shoulder, sometimes tied sashlike around her waist, and, rarely, wrapped around her head like a turban. She also wore lots of large silver rings, which I knew would make my mother sniff with disapproval and my older sister Alice laugh. But I thought they were kind of cool.

Kat left her lunch untouched. I ate mine, but I didn't really taste it.

"I'm in love with her," I announced to Kat.

Kat gulped her soda. "I noticed," she said, burping.

I looked at her severely. "Pistols or swords?"

"Huh?"

I shrugged. "If we're rivals," I told her, only half joking, "we'll have to have a duel." I know that sounds weird, but we'd read a lot of swashbuckling books as kids, and the guys in them were always having duels.

Kat gave me a funny look and stood up. "Penny," she said, picking up her tray, "we are not rivals."

"Why not?" I drew my imaginary sword and slashed at the air.

"Because . . ." Kat balanced her tray on one arm and matched me blow for blow with her own invisible weapon. "Oh, just because. See you at tryouts."

Cross-country tryouts were that afternoon. My grandmother had been a track runner when she was a kid, and she'd started me running when I was around eight; she even used to race me sometimes. I had plenty of experience both on the roads and in the woods, and I felt pretty confident I'd get on at least the junior varsity. Gramma, who was my biggest fan, said there was no reason why I shouldn't. "At least there isn't if those fancy coaches today know anything," she told me. Gramma had almost qualified for the Olympics back in the 1950s, and she had a lot of negative stuff to say about how things are done now. Mom sometimes called her a crusty old lady, mostly joking about it, but Gramma's occasional crustiness was okay with me. She was just about the most important person in my life along with my parents and Kat; Kat loved her too.

Kat, by the way, had been running for precisely three months, eighteen days, and—she reminded me when we reported to the track for tryouts—fourteen hours.

"There she is," I whispered as Megan and the coach, Mrs. Larrimew, strode up to the bench where we were all huddled; they were in earnest conversation. Then Megan tossed her corn-silk hair and laughed, sending shivers down my spine. She'd braided the blue-and-yellow scarf into her hair where it was close to her head, and left it hanging free where her hair was against her back.

"What's the matter, Penny?" Kat asked. "You cold or something?" She gave my shoulders a rub.

I shook my head, pushed her hand away, and nodded toward where Megan was now standing in front of us with Coach Larrimew, eyeing us as if we were inferior cuts of meat at a deli counter.

"Oh," Kat said.

"Listen up, ladies." Coach Larrimew launched into a pretty standard beginning-of-the-year-type speech about sportsmanship and The Schedule and what we were going to do that afternoon.

What we were going to do was have a sort of mock race on the course we'd all walked the day before: through the woods in back of the school, across the football field, which the boys' coach had promised not to use till later that afternoon, and ending with two laps around the track. Megan and a couple of the other seniors on varsity would be running with us to check us out, and Coach Larrimew would time us.

Megan handed out numbers and actually pinned them on a couple of kids. I tried to ease over to where she was so I'd be one of them, but before I got very far, Kat grabbed a couple of numbers and pinned one on me.

"Thanks," I said sarcastically.

"What?" Kat looked surprised. She turned around and handed me her number.

Luckily Coach Larrimew blew her whistle and motioned us to line up, cutting off my nasty reply about Kat's not having the sensitivity to notice I'd wanted to get my number from Megan. Begrudgingly I pinned Kat's on, crooked, and sprinted to the starting line, as close to Megan as I could get.

It wasn't long before I broke ahead of Kat; she'd been laboring from the first and I could see that she was having trouble navigating roots and rocks. "You go on," she panted, waving me ahead when we'd been in the woods for less than ten minutes. I gave her a wave back and picked up my pace. I could see Megan in front of us running with the leaders, but not so far away that I couldn't catch them, I was pretty sure.

I surged forward; the ground was pretty rough, with big roots crossing the path, and loose pebbles, not to mention wet pine needles and rocks. I had my eyes on Megan; there was no one close behind me, although I could hear kids coming.

And then, my eyes still on Megan, my foot slipped on the edge of a rock, and I went down, banging my knee on the way.

Tears stung my eyes, as much from embarrassment as from pain, but then a hand—a smooth, gracefully beringed hand—reached down to mine and pulled me up till my face was within inches of . . . Megan's!

"Keep your eyes open, Johnson, Jackson, whatever your name is," she said. "That'll cost you time."

I nodded, blinking the tears back and rubbing my knee. Then I realized I was still gripping her hand and she was trying to pull it loose.

I let go, reluctantly, but not before I'd noticed her clean, perfectly shaped nails and seen that one of her silver rings had a tiny four-leaf clover dangling from it. "Th-thanks," I managed to say, but by then she was already gone.

Someone came up behind me, panting like she'd just run a marathon. Then Kat's hand was on my shoulder. "You okay?" she gasped.

"Yeah, I—I guess so," I said, still looking after Megan.

Kat gave me a little push from behind. "Then you'd better get going if you want to get on the team. Go on—scram."

* * *

I did qualify, but only just. I had the slowest time of those who did, which embarrassed me when I told Gramma. But when I told her about the fall, she said not to worry about my time but to worry about my eyes, meaning I should look where I was going instead of at whoever was ahead or behind me. At least I was able to tell her I'd made up some of the time on the track at the end, even though my knee had begun to puff up.

"Here," Megan had said in the locker room after tryouts, tossing something that looked like a limp soccer ball to Kat. "Make Johnson put this on her knee."

Kat, who hadn't qualified but was hanging around anyway, handed me the limp soccer ball, which turned out to be an ice bag.

"Thanks," I called. "It's Jackson, by the way. Penny Jackson."

Megan sort of smiled at me as she left. I think she also said "Whatever," but I might be wrong about that.

"How's your knee?" Kat asked.

"Okay," I lied. "Wasn't she great?"

"Who?"

I looked at her, astonished. "Megan, of course! Didn't you see her flying around the track at the end?"

"Nope." Kat gathered up her running clothes and stuffed them into her backpack. "You're the only one I saw flying around the track at the end."

"But Megan—"

"See you outside," Kat said. "At the late bus. If you hurry."

"Yeah, okay." But I iced my knee for a few more minutes, reveling in the fact that Megan had gotten the bag for me, and in the memory of her hair and her scarf streaming out behind her as she ran, with her white shorts and singlet shining in the early autumn sun.

I was sure Gramma'd be impressed with her too, but she just gave me a look when I described Megan to her. "Handsome is as handsome does," she muttered crustily. "Watch her *technique*, Penny, if she's so good." Then she gave me a funny look—well, a penetrating look maybe. "How come she doesn't know your name?"

"I'm only a freshman," I told her. "It's the beginning of the year."

"*Humph!*" Gramma grunted.

Kat and I had always done the same things together. I was better at some and she was better at others, but that was okay; the one who was better had always helped the one who wasn't so good. That fall, since Kat was determined to make the team next year, I coached her in cross country, and she read the stuff I tried to write for the literary magazine.

Of course I wrote about Megan.

She walks in beauty like the day was how I began the poem I hoped would make it into the magazine.

"Derivative," Kat said promptly when I slid the first line onto her desk in homeroom.

"Huh?"

"Derivative. Like someone else's poem. Lord Byron's, for example. 'She walks in beauty, like the night.' "

I groaned and went back to my desk.

Megan, Reagan, pagan . . . I scribbled, thinking maybe I'd better try for something that rhymed. *Beggin', Bacon* (NO!), *Fagan, leggin'* . . . Well, I thought, I don't have to rhyme with her name, after all.

Finally I came up with this:

> *Your beauty is like the sun and the stars and the moon.*
> *You walk with grace untold.*
> *Your lips are two parentheses surrounding your mouth's*
>   *pink cave,*
> *Home to the whitest of teeth, the most silver of tongues.*
> *Your voice is sweeter than birdsong,*
> *And when you run,*
> *Dust motes dance before you, carving your way through*
>   *the air,*
> *And the swiftness of birds is in your footsteps.*

Kat studied my poem for a very long time without saying anything.

"No good, huh?" I asked anxiously, reading over her shoulder. "It's free verse, of course. But you got that, right?"

"Yes," Kat said. "I got that."

It did seem a little clumsy now that I was looking at it through Kat's eyes.

Kat licked her lips. "It's not *no* good," she said carefully. "It's got—it's got some good—er—some good bits in it. Like . . ."

I snatched my poem away. "It's okay," I said gruffly. "You don't have to sputter."

Kat grabbed my hand. "Oh, Penn, I'm sorry! It *does* have good bits in it. The last line, for instance, and—and 'sweeter than birdsong' and some other lines. Maybe you could work on it some more, but . . ." Her eyes were filled with all the sincerity and honesty and friendship and kindness that I'd always loved and admired in her. "Penn, it's pretty obvious it's a love poem to a girl," she said finally. "So it might not be such a great idea to send it to the magazine, especially since everyone kind of knows how you feel about Megan."

"Everyone?" I asked, feeling cold inside. "And what do you mean how *I* feel? We both feel that way, don't we? Hmmm? Don't we?"

"Well, to tell you the truth," Kat said, sounding like my mom's best friend, who said that all the time, "no. I—I like Megan, I think. I mean she's pretty and all, but—"

"Fine," I said, slamming my hand down on Kat's desk and turning away. "Fine. I'll write something bland that no one'll get."

"Try symbolism," Kat suggested softly.

So I did, once I'd cooled off. I wrote a sappy poem about strands of corn silk leading down to luscious yellow kernels, sweet and plump and juicy. Kat looked embarrassed when she read it, but the magazine accepted it, and when it was published, a junior came up to me and said, "That's the sexiest poem I've ever read in this magazine."

"I'll be writing porn next," I quipped, but inside I glowed.

From then on it got easier. I wrote lots of flower poems and fruit poems, and once in a while I slipped a really good one into Megan's locker, unsigned. Okay, I guess it was stupid of me to think she wouldn't know who'd written those poems, but I couldn't help myself. Besides, Megan had really been smiling at me now and then in practice. Once she yelled, "Pick up your feet, Johnson, for God's sake, or you'll fall again!" which, despite the wrong name, I considered a valuable running tip.

One morning Kat handed me this:

> My love knows my love not and is so blind,
> She sees not my true heart nor aching mind.
> My love is swift; her grace is like the deer's,
> But swifter is her blindness to my tears.
> Her eyes turn elsewhere and she sees me not;
> With pain and sadness my poor heart is shot.

So, shadow-like, I wait and watch and pray
In dismal hope my words will find a way
To melt her heart. Oh, bring her gaze around,
And show her that in me, true love is found!

"Well, what do you think?" she asked. Her face was very pink, and her eyes were anxious.

"I think it's pistols or swords again," I told her after a couple of minutes during which I realized (1) that it was much better than anything I could ever write, and (2) that I was jealous and mad.

"Huh?"

"You heard me," I said. "We're rivals again."

"We're *what*? Oh my God!" Kat clapped her hand to her head. "It's not about Megan, you dork! It's . . ." Her pink face turned bright red, and she stormed down the hall.

Later, at lunch, I asked Kat who the poem was about and if she was going to send it to the literary magazine.

"I don't think so," she answered, toying with her food and avoiding, now that I think of it, the first part of my question. "It still needs work, for one thing. And I'd have to change the pronouns."

I grinned. "Or your name. How about Anonymous?"

"Yeah." Kat snapped a celery stalk in two as if she were

trying to execute it. "That fits me perfectly. Anonymous. A. Nonny Mouse."

Her voice sounded weird—bitter, really—and she looked as if she was going to cry, so I brushed her hand with mine. "What's wrong, Katty?"

She just shook her head bravely and changed the subject to the fall dance that was going to be held at the end of the month.

I dreaded that dance. I mean, I can't dance worth beans anyway, and I knew enough about myself at that point to know I didn't want to go with a boy. Heck, I didn't even want to *dance* with a boy; I wanted to dance with Megan. I didn't want to put a label on how I felt, even though I was pretty sure I knew what label would fit—especially when Kat pointed out a poster in the hall announcing the first meeting of the school's gay-straight alliance.

"So what?" I said, wishing my stomach hadn't suddenly started to do gymnastics exercises.

"Well, I thought I might go. Would you come with me?"

I shrugged.

"You don't have to be gay to go," she said quickly, running her finger along the place where the poster said ALL WELCOME— GAY, BI, STRAIGHT, QUESTIONING.

"I can read," I said.

Okay, that was mean, but the poster and Kat's wanting both

of us to go to the meeting annoyed me in a way I didn't want to think about.

"Well, I might go anyway," Kat said.

We left it at that.

I did go to the dance, though; my mom made me, and Gramma kept saying it couldn't hurt even if I did have to dance with a boy. "Boys don't bite, Penny," she said. "At least not most of them. Some of them are even nice. Like your grandfather, after all, and your daddy."

I had to admit she was right about Grandpa and Dad, but even so, that didn't make me eager to go. Mom kept telling me what fun my sister Alice always had at dances, but hey, I'm not Alice, you know?

Mom drove me there, with Kat. We didn't have dates, thank God. I figured we'd sit in a corner and watch everyone else having a wonderful time.

Ha! Sure.

Only moments after Mom had left us at the door and chirped, "Have a lovely time, girls! See you at eleven," Megan arrived.

And naturally she wasn't dropped off by her mom. No, no, Megan came floating in on the arm of Chris Pollack, who even I knew was the school's star football player. Chris had on skintight black pants and a red shirt I could die for, with most of its buttons undone, and Megan had on a sleeveless, slinky, green minidress, the bottom of which was cut in sort of scallops, only instead of being rounded they were pointed, making her look like a mermaid dressed in strips of that long green seaweed—kelp, I think it's called. The scarf clung to the front of her neck so its two ends hung down her back, her corn-silk hair puffed over her shoulders, and huge trashy gold earrings dangled on either side of her face. Gold and green and black bangles encircled both her arms almost to the elbows.

I couldn't take my eyes off her, and I hated Chris with every fiber of my being.

That was when I realized I probably *should* plan to go to that gay-straight alliance meeting. I lay awake all night after the dance, imagining myself making out with Megan the way I'd seen Chris doing in his car when Kat and I were waiting for Mom. It embarrasses me to say it, but I touched myself the way I knew Chris had probably been touching Megan. I liked the way that made me feel, but even so, it was frustrating and lonely with only me doing it.

Afterward I had a weird dream, but all I remember is that Megan and Kat were both in it and that when I woke up, I was all sweaty.

We had our first cross-country meet not long after that. I managed to stay in the lead pack with Megan almost the whole way, even though now that I'd seen her with Chris, I knew she was probably never going to notice me the way I now knew I wanted to be noticed. Still, it was great emerging from the woods with Megan and the other leaders, hearing Kat's voice and Gramma's screaming, "Go, Penny, go!" and feeling Megan's hand slap my back when we'd both crossed the finish line. "Good going, kid," Megan said, turning her head toward mine; we were both bent over, hands on knees, getting our breath back.

"Thanks," I said, glowing.

That night Gramma told me she agreed with me that Megan was pretty. "Handsome does fine in her case, Penny," she said, "as far as running goes, anyway. Her form is as gorgeous as the rest of her, and she runs like a dream. So do you, by the way. You've come a long way."

That made me tingle with happiness, but it was as much what Gramma said about Megan that pleased me as it was what she said about me.

Gramma gave me one of her funny looks. "You like her a lot, don't you?"

I nodded, and Gramma nodded too, thoughtfully, as if she understood.

Later, in my room, instead of going to sleep, I wrote a poem about a palomino mare outrunning a thoroughbred stallion, and I put it in Megan's locker the next day.

That afternoon at dismissal when I went to my own locker

to get my books before practice, I saw Megan standing at hers with Chris; she was showing him a piece of paper and giggling.

Ignoring Chris, I said, "Hi, Megan, going to practice?"

Megan looked up, grinned at Chris, and said, *"Um,"* loudly, to him, not to me.

Chris laughed and called, "Hey, baby butch! You're the stallion, right?"

Megan laughed then, the same laugh as before. It sent chills down my spine again, but this time they were bad chills, and I realized what the paper must be. Without thinking, I snatched it out of Megan's hand and ran past my locker, past Kat, who had just come into the hall, past the door to the gym locker rooms, and outside, where I ran home faster than I'd ever run in practice.

Then I threw myself on my bed and cried till Gramma came into my room and held me while I told her everything. "Oh baby," she said, all her crustiness gone. "It's not the end of the world. Just"—here she tipped my face up and smiled into my eyes—"just be careful who you love."

I moaned something about no one loving me back, and Gramma shook her head. The crustiness returned a little, or firmness anyway, when she said, "Uh-uh, Penny, don't waste your time in self-pity. You lose a race, you lose a love, you pick yourself up and go on. There are more races and more loves waiting around the corner." She patted my shoulder. "That Megan may be a good runner, but maybe that's all she is."

* * *

"Megan was just trying to impress Chris," I said stubbornly to Kat on the phone that night when I'd calmed down enough to talk about it. "Maybe she wants him to write poems to her and he won't, and maybe she'll realize that I can, and maybe . . ." I couldn't think of what that might lead to, though, so I stopped.

"Penny." Kat's voice was so soft and gentle I barely heard it. "Penny, she's straight. She—"

"I know." I cut her off, too upset to even pretend to argue against the implication that I was probably gay. "I know. But maybe she isn't *really* straight. And she likes me, Kat, I know that. She thinks I'm a good runner. She—she . . ."

I could hear Kat sighing on the other end of the phone. "I know," she said. "She gave you a running tip, and she smiles at you sometimes. But—"

I cut her off again. "I'm pretty sure Megan and I could be— friends, at least," I said. "It's just going to take time, that's all. Time and patience."

"Okay, Penn." Kat's voice sounded sad, somehow. "If that's what you want."

I didn't put any more poems in Megan's locker after that, but I wrote plenty. Sometimes I showed them to Kat, but most of the time I didn't. I started going for long runs after practice till Mom complained that it was getting too dark for that to be safe. But I got so my time was almost as good as Megan's, and our team began to get a reputation as being the best in our district. We won meet after meet, and Megan began including me in her strategy talks with the other leaders. Sometimes she even sat next to me on the bus going to or from races. Okay, so when she wasn't talking strategy, she usually slept or sang along with everyone else, so it wasn't as if we had any intimate moments. But I liked sitting next to her, especially feeling her slightly damp body next to mine after a race. Kat had become assistant manager, so she was usually with us. But I didn't always make a big effort to sit with her if I saw Megan coming my way.

One Friday night when my parents and Gramma and I were having supper—codfish cakes and baked beans, not exactly my favorite—Gramma suddenly put her hand up to her head and said, "Sorry—I think I'd better be excused. I've got a terrible headache." She stood up, sort of swaying. Mom looked at Dad and said, "I'll get you some aspirin, Momma. You just stay put."

"No," Gramma said, "don't trouble . . ."

And then before Mom could reach her, Gramma melted into a heap on the floor.

The emergency-room doctor said Gramma had had a stroke and was unconscious. They were going to admit her, but they had to do some tests or wait for an empty bed or something first, so Mom and Dad and I all sat there holding hands in the waiting room, worrying and trying not to cry.

Finally I asked, "Can I call Kat?" Mom said, "Of course," and Kat and her mom were there in about twenty minutes. Mrs. Rogers talked to Mom and Dad, and Kat and I went outside.

Kat held both my hands so tight I thought they'd break while I told her what had happened. But I didn't mind; it was as if the strength of her grip was making me stronger.

She and her mom stayed with us till long after the hospital had admitted Gramma into intensive care. Finally Mrs. Rogers and Kat drove me home so I could get my pjs, and then took me to their house, where I spent the night sitting on the window seat in Kat's room, staring out at the stars and talking about Gramma while Kat sat next to me and rubbed my back.

The next couple of days are pretty much a blur in my mind. Mom's sister—my aunt Judy—and her husband, Uncle Larry, flew across the country from New Mexico, where they live, and my sister Alice came home from college, and we all spent most of our time at the hospital. Mrs. Rogers dropped Kat off there both Saturday and Sunday morning and she and I took lots of long, sad walks around the hospital's neighborhood. I remember seeing an old lady raking leaves outside one of the houses, and I hated her because she was so well and Gramma was so sick.

On Sunday night they let me see her. She had her mouth open and her eyes shut and she was breathing very slowly, and she had tubes in her and cords like electric wires going from her to machines. At first I couldn't take my eyes off them. But then I thought, no, that stuff's got nothing to do with Gramma, and when Mom left me alone with her, I sat there holding Gramma's hand and telling her what a good person she was and what a good runner and what an inspiration she was to me and how much I loved her. And I told her that I'd run every race for her and that I'd try to remember what she'd said about losing races and there being other ones around the corner. Then I remembered she'd said that about losing loves too.

After a while a nurse came in and told me I had to leave, so I gave Gramma a kiss and told her again that I loved her, and then I smoothed her soft, almost-white hair back off her forehead and left.

Later that same night, Gramma died.

The next day I couldn't go to school; I mostly slept and then went with Mom and Dad and Alice and Aunt Judy and Uncle Larry to the funeral home. I waited till after everyone else had gone up to Gramma's casket, and then I slipped in a couple of the ribbons she'd won and had given to me. I kept one for myself, but somehow I felt she ought to have the others with her wherever she was going.

The day after that Mom made me go to school, but I don't remember anything about my classes except that Kat sat next to me in most of them and poked me when we had to do something like open a book or write.

After school I ran to the funeral home to have a few minutes with Gramma before practice; I figured there'd be time. But I guess I stayed longer than I should have because when I got back, the team had finished stretching and was already on one of the woods paths we used sometimes. I caught up with them pretty quickly and was just about to say "Sorry I'm late" to Megan when she turned around and gave me a really black look. Then she surged ahead as if she didn't want to have anything to do with me.

In the locker room after practice, Megan came up to where I was changing my shoes; Kat, who'd come in to walk home with me, was sitting next to me on the bench. Megan's corn-silk hair was out of its scrunchy and tangled around her shoulders, and she looked really mad. "Johnson," she said quietly, like she was forcing herself not to yell, "you've turned into a good runner. But we don't need prima donnas on our team. We need people to come to practice every day—on time. Got that? This is a warning."

I felt tears fill my eyes, but I was too numb to do anything except look up at her stupidly.

Kat wasn't numb. She stood up, facing Megan, and she said,

"For the hundredth time, Megan, her name is Jackson, not Johnson. And she missed practice yesterday and was late today because her grandmother died. You'd be a better captain if you tried to get to know people before you yelled at them."

Megan looked startled. But then she recovered and snapped, "Well, JACKson, that's a bummer. But life has to go on. So does this team. We're all part of it, even you. And if you can't be here, you'd better call. Those are the rules. Follow them."

She wheeled and stalked away.

I lost it then. I completely lost it. I hadn't cried since we were all at the hospital that first night, and now it was as if three days' worth of tears brimmed up inside me and spewed out.

Kat shooed everyone else out of the locker room and put her arms around me. "Shhh," she said. "It's okay, Penny, it's okay. Let it out, go ahead and cry. Shh, Penny, shh, my love, my dearest love, it's okay. . . ."

I clung to her, sobbing so hard it took a long time for her words to reach me.

But when they finally did, what Gramma had said about new races and new loves came back to me, and it finally hit me that I'd been too stupidly starry-eyed over Megan to see that there was an old love waiting for me much closer than around the corner.

I looked at Kat and saw those gentle puppy-dog eyes of hers looking softly into mine.

"What?" I whispered. "What did you call me?"

"Love," she whispered back, and I could see tears in her eyes too. "I called you love." Very slowly, Kat moved her head closer to mine, and before I was really aware of what was happening, I was kissing her and she was kissing me. The knowledge that I'd almost thrown Kat away swept over me like an immense tidal wave.

"It's us," I said, "isn't it?"

Kat moved back a little and smiled at me. "Yes, Penny," she said. "It always has been. You just didn't figure it out till now."

"Katherine Emily Rogers," I said, "I love you." And Gramma, I added silently, you were so right. Handsome is as handsome does.

"I love you too, Penny," Kat said, pulling out a tissue and using it to wipe my eyes and then hers.

And I knew that from then on, always, it would be Kat.

ABOUT NANCY GARDEN

The author of more than twenty-five books, Nancy Garden finds her inspiration for stories and characters everywhere, sometimes even in the events of her own life and those of others. Her award-winning novel *Annie on My Mind* broke ground for its honest portrayal of a lesbian relationship and coming-out experience. Controversy over the novel plunged Nancy into a fierce censorship battle and in part inspired her 1999 novel about censorship, *The Year They Burned the Books*. Nancy's other acclaimed novels include *Lark in the Morning*, *The Loners*, *Dove and Sword: A Novel of Joan of Arc*, *Good Moon Rising*, and *Holly's Secret*. Her work on censorship issues led to her receiving the 2000 Robert B. Downs Intellectual Freedom Award.

She writes, "I'm a hopeless romantic! My partner Sandy and I just celebrated our thirty-third anniversary, but we met when we were both twelve, sitting on top of the parallel bars on our school playground. We didn't get to know each other, though, until we were in high school and both rehearsing one-act plays. I remember standing with Sandy under a streetlight, waiting for my mother to pick us up, and talking with her very seriously about acting and singing but feeling oh so deeply that something special was happening that was going to change my life forever. And of course, it did! That moment under the streetlight was the beginning of a love that has been the focus of my life. Desire? That too, of course."

ONE HOT SECOND

RACHEL VAIL

ABOUT A month ago I dumped this kid named George. He cried in the cafeteria. It was horrible. I almost said I'd go back out with him right then and there, just to get him to stop. I can't handle scenes. But I didn't like George anymore. I liked a kid named Kevin. A week after I dumped George, Kevin asked me out and of course I said yes.

There is one problem with Kevin. He's a little fast. He French-kissed his last girlfriend twelve times at one dance, but I tried not to let it bother me. I really wanted to kiss him and I knew he wanted to kiss me, but I didn't know he was horny enough to want to do it in the hall.

Well, a week after I started going out with Kevin, I found myself standing in the hall between fifth and sixth block with my arms around him and my tongue in his mouth. It was really disgusting but I liked it.

It was my first kiss.

I'd had this idea about waiting and George respected that. He might have thought it was weird but he never acted that way. He just said he respected that I was an independent thinker and pure person and he would wait until I was ready. George is a real gentleman. Mothers like George. Good old George.

Anyway, I got sick of waiting. I couldn't remember what exactly I was waiting for. I wanted to kiss somebody and fall in love. My twin sister, Meredith, has fallen in love with all three boys she's kissed, and she said there was no way I could possibly understand how awesome and overpowering that kind of love is without experiencing it for myself. She said it was beyond describing. I realized that in my entire life every single experience had been describable. In fact, I'd described most of them to Meredith.

I had some romantic ideas about how my first kiss would happen. Maybe there'd be a willow tree, maybe some music. Kissing George would've been like kissing my cousin. Totally describable. Plus, I didn't want to tell him "Forget all that stuff I've been saying for a year—I want to kiss now." He'd think I was horny and not as interesting and different and pure as he'd imagined. I didn't want to disappoint George.

Kevin scrunches his eyes when he looks at you. He leans close. The day before I dumped George, Kevin had stopped me in the hall and asked if I was ready for the bio quiz. While he was asking, he touched my hair. It was a strand on the front left side. He twirled it around his index finger and then let go. When he did that, I couldn't remember if I was even taking bio this year. I think I may actually have said "duh." Kevin smiled and strolled into class. I sat down on the floor and realized I had to dump George.

The only reason it took me until the next day to do the dumping was because I was too stupid to talk, and way weak in the legs for the rest of that afternoon.

Two weeks later I was pressed up against a locker kissing Kevin. The lock was digging into my backbone, but I didn't want to wreck my first kiss by readjusting. I squeezed my eyes shut and tried to concentrate.

I wanted to be mature and focus on the kiss, but even beyond the stabbing pain in my back, I was really distracted by wondering what kind of sicko invented French kissing. I'm not even supposed to share a bottle of water with anyone because of germs.

When we finished kissing, I had to wipe my mouth dry. We didn't say good-bye or anything. I took the gum off the back of my hand and put it in my mouth. Luckily there was some mint flavor left because the taste in my mouth was a little mildewy. I thought, Maybe this is what Kevin's mouth always tastes like to him. That idea made me gag a bit. I tried to concentrate on the mintiness and also on the fact that it was the kind of gum that supposedly kills the germs that cause bad breath, so I thought, Well, maybe it will kill whatever germs Kevin might've given me. That nauseated me even more.

The bell was ringing, so I ran to class, hoping nobody had seen, or at least not too many people. Maybe a few, because people had been saying I was a little weird, the whole not-kissing thing, and being in ninth grade already.

Apparently people saw. And talked. All my teachers found out about it, and on the following Monday I was taken out of my gym class to go talk with Mr. Herman, the head ninth-grade teacher. Mr. Herman scares me because he's so hairy. Everybody calls him Mr. Hair-man. I think it's mean but I call him that too. Not to his face, of course. One kid supposedly made a mistake and called him Mr. Hair-man to his face last year and got suspended for a week, which goes on your permanent record.

So I was walking down the hall with Mr. Hair-man and I almost started to crack up because my hand brushed against his paw by mistake. But by the time we got to his room I had calmed myself down.

"Mallory," he said. "There has been a rumor going around that you and your boyfriend, Kevin, engaged in a kiss last Thursday. Is this correct?" he asked.

"Yes," I barely said. It felt so weird. Nobody had called Kevin my *boyfriend* before. My boyfriend. Mr. Hair-man was the first to make it official.

Then he went on to tell me that kissing was not a proper thing to do in school. I agreed with him, nodding. Then he said, "I'm going to have to call your mother."

That did it. I hadn't even told my mother I was going out with anybody. I started to shake and there were tears running down my face. I never wanted my mother to know anything about my private life because I knew I would get The Talk. I was bawling. The worst part was that Mr. Hair-man was pulling out Kleenex and handing them to me one at a time with his hairy hand. He came around his desk and sat on the edge, telling me he wasn't trying to be mean.

Yeah, well, your Nobel Peace Prize is in the mail.

I said I was sorry and asked if I could go to the bathroom.

He said, "By all means."

I spent the whole rest of the block in the stall crying. When the bell rang, I tried to pull myself together and move on with my day, but as soon as I hit the hall, Meredith saw me and asked, "What's wrong?" I was instantly bawling again. We rushed back into the bathroom. All my friends came in and we spent the period in there, me telling them what happened and them backing me up. Even Diandra, who was Kevin's last girlfriend who got kissed the twelve times, was sympathetic. She gets in trouble all the time, so she said if I got grounded and wanted to know how to climb out my window, I should call her. She's not one of my closest friends, but she's sort of trying to shift over from the smokers to our group. I don't mind. I don't look down on someone just because of how much makeup she wears.

It was so hard to go to lunch because I could feel all the eyes on me, especially Kevin's. I couldn't eat. My best friend, Anne, put her straw in my 7-Up but I couldn't drink, either, and anyway, there was the germ issue. I felt sick enough that I'd already gotten Kevin's germs; I didn't want to add Anne's, too. Meredith tossed my lunch for me and we all just went out to the courtyard and ignored the boys.

When I got home, my mother was waiting for me. Meredith tried to stick around, but Mom sent her up to our room and then she said, "Mallory! I cannot believe! How in the world?"

I just stood there. It takes my mother a while to get going.

"Kissing in the hall? In the *hall*?" Like the big issue was the location. Like if it had been the cafeteria, no problem.

"Oh, Mother," I said. "Don't be ridiculous. I would never." I went past her to the fridge. I was hungry after no lunch at all. I took a plum and started devouring it. It was really good and juicy.

"Mr. Herman called me at work," Mom said. "He said it was urgent. So there I was, in the middle of an important meeting, with everybody, including my boss, eavesdropping while Mr. Herman says that my daughter Mallory has been caught making out in the hall!"

I opened a 7-Up, closed the fridge, and sat on a stool at the breakfast bar. "He has no idea," I said, popping the plum pit into my mouth.

"Well," said Mom, reopening the fridge and getting herself a 7-Up too. "Was it that nice George?"

The 7-Up was too bubbly; it made my eyes water. I rested my head on the breakfast bar and let my mother talk. Talk, talk, talk. Appropriate times, some things are private, love can be beautiful when blah, blah, blah. Exactly what I had been trying to avoid.

I spat out the plum pit and left, but even that didn't slow Mom down. She followed me all the way to the bathroom, talk, talk, talking, and then sat on the floor while I filled a Dixie cup and threw two Tylenols down my throat. I leaned against the sink and eventually slid down the cabinet. Mom was still lecturing me, so I clamped my head between my knees and folded my arms over my head. Reputation, self-respect. Why should he buy a cow.

"What?"

My mother shook her head and said it was an expression her mother used to use, never mind.

"Why should *who* buy a cow?" We live in the suburbs. Nobody has a cow.

"Nobody. George. So was it George?"

"Am I the cow?"

"Oh, Mallory," Mom groaned. "Forget the cow. Do you understand what I'm telling you?"

The only unexpected thing she had said was "Why should he buy a cow," and it was obvious she wasn't going to explain that. I had to escape. I have a problem with boredom. It bores me. Violently. So I said, "Yes, thank you, I'm sorry." All the words she likes.

Mom gave me a kiss on the hair and I was free to go. Hallelujah. When I got to our room, Meredith asked how The Talk was and I pretended to throw up. Meredith, who has been kissing since seventh grade—three separate boys—has never gotten The Talk. Meredith has defenses.

Everybody was e-mailing was I grounded and was mine and my sister's party for Friday night canceled, but luckily my mother hadn't thought of doing that, so the party was still on. Diandra seemed disappointed that I didn't need to learn how to climb out my window and invited me to come over and climb out hers. I typed GTG and signed off.

All night as I was trying to sleep, I was thinking about the kiss. First I was thinking about how much trouble it had caused, and how unfair it was that I of all people would get in trouble for kissing in school when I am such a prude.

114

Then I was thinking, Maybe it was worth it.

I can't say the tongue part was good. It may just be one of those things you have to get used to, like other French stuff. Cream sauces. Hairy armpits. My mother went to France for a year in college, and after a few months she got used to those things and the weird way you have to say R sounds. On the other hand, I still don't like French toast. I eat cereal when my mother and sister have it for breakfast, humming about how good it is. I may turn out to be a person who doesn't acquire tastes or who is anti-French. There are probably plenty of adults who don't enjoy French kissing.

Actually, it is absolutely nauseating to imagine any adult I know enjoying French kissing.

I could hardly keep from gagging, remembering I did it myself. It had felt like a fish. A live, muscular fish swimming around in my mouth. I wiggled my tongue around to try to re-create the moment. It didn't work. I folded it over and sucked but that still wasn't exactly it. Then my tongue started feeling too big for my mouth. What a weird thing a tongue is.

But beyond that and the germs, there was something nice about the moment of the kiss. I'm not sure if it was pressing the front of me into the front of Kevin, or his hands gripping my shoulders, or his warm breath on my cheek. I closed my eyes in the dark of my room and tried to remember all the details. I think part of what I liked was the way my neck stretched as my head bent back. I tipped my chin up toward the ceiling. Not sure why that felt so good, but it really did. I touched my neck. Now there's a part of me I never particularly noticed before. My neck. The skin was soft. Maybe I have a nice neck. Maybe next time we kiss, Kevin will touch my neck and fall in love with me because of it. I resolved to do neck-stretching exercises every night. I looked over at Meredith to see if her neck looked the same as mine. Her fist was balled up under her chin, protecting it. I hoped my neck was better.

I closed my eyes to get away from my sister and back to Kevin and remembering. Part of my brain was warning, Don't try to describe each tiny detail or you'll ruin the indescribableness, but the rest of my brain couldn't help pushing ahead, going over and over that moment, putting it into words so I'd never lose my grip on it. I may be too talkative to ever fall in love.

Might he have been humming? I definitely didn't notice humming at the time of the kiss, but as I lay in my bed trying to relive it, I kept hearing this little sighing hum in my mind the second before his lips touched mine. I am ninety to ninety-five percent sure Kevin hummed, or else he definitely sighed. Nobody ever told me about that part. Maybe that's what always happens. The boy sighs a private little hum-sigh only the about-to-be-kissed girl can hear. Oh, that has to be the most romantic thing. I hope I wasn't supposed to make a private noise too. No, Meredith definitely would have told me if I had to make a noise. She would've made me practice.

I pulled the blankets up to my nose and tried to imitate

Kevin's sound myself. Meredith grumbled in her sleep. I flipped over and pressed myself against the mattress, pretending I was kissing Kevin instead of my Dolphins pillow. Now I get it, I thought, now that I've had the experience myself. I am falling, almost indescribably, in love.

The next morning Kevin passed me in the hall. I pretended not to notice him and then, walking into homeroom, I made sure to completely ignore him, not wanting to make a fool of myself in case I was more in love than he was. My face was so hot my ears burned as I passed him in the hall before English. My first love. It was so exciting I thought I might literally pass out.

Then before fourth block one of the boys told Meredith that Kevin thought I was a slut and so did all the teachers. Meredith pointed out that if I was a slut, then so was Kevin. She was right, but it hurt anyway. Why would he think that? He seemed to like me enough the day before. When I passed him on my way to fifth block, he looked at me, and not in a falling-in-love way. More like a hating way. I lost it.

Anne and Meredith raced behind me back to the bathroom. "How—how could he think . . . ," I sputtered.

Meredith was all hostile, ready to take on all the boys in my defense. She had found the hole in their logic and was ready to destroy them with it. Logic was *so* not the point, but you can't explain that to Meredith once she gets psyched about being right in an argument, so to get her off it I said, "And the teachers, too? What in the world does that mean?"

Anne said, "Don't worry, the teachers couldn't know. They don't know anything."

I pointed out that obviously at least Mr. Hair-man knew.

"That's true," Anne said, nodding thoughtfully. "Do you think they talk about us in the teacher's lounge?"

I groaned.

"Well, even if they do," Meredith reasoned, grabbing some toilet paper for me to blow my nose, "There's no way a teacher would be gossiping with the ninth-grade boys."

Anne jumped up and said, "That's right! Like can't you just see Mr. Hair-man going up to the boys and being like, 'Hey, guys! Ms. Kilbane and Mrs. Rhone and I all think Mallory is such a slut now, don't you?' "

Meredith laughed. Anne is very good at imitating. I know Anne meant to help, but her theatrical gifts are not always so comforting.

"Yes," Anne continued in Ms. Kilbane's Chicago accent. "Mallory the slut."

Me, a slut. One week I'm a stuck-up prude, then suddenly I'm a slut? In one kiss? It's one thing for Diandra to be called a slut. She does a lot more than kiss, everybody says. But me?

"I don't think so," Meredith said, which stopped Anne's performance. "OK?"

"OK." I washed my face and put on some fresh eyeliner. Then I went over it again; I even filled the inner rims, like Diandra does. I looked different. Kind of cheap. I flipped my hair, blinked a few times, looking in the mirror, and then went to English. I was trying hard to make my face seem tough and mysterious. My English teacher, Ms. Kilbane, shook her head at me as she passed out the quiz. I swear it, she shook her head like she was disappointed, like I'd ruined everything, all her expectations. I only got six out of ten, I was so messed up. And I'd completely studied.

I passed notes to Meredith and Anne saying *I hate Kevin.* They didn't blame me. I added that they could pass the message along. They did, in the hall after. Everybody wanted to know if I was breaking up with Kevin or if he was he breaking up with me.

"Either way," I said, slamming my locker. "As long as we're *done.*"

It seemed like the right thing to do, but deep down I knew I still loved him. I've gone out with boys before, like good old George, but Kevin was the first one I ever French-kissed, and that is special. It means something. When I was going out with George, I'd forget about him all day until he popped up in front of me. Kevin crowded out absolutely everything. I felt all twitchy and sweaty and cold, like my heart was beating way too fast for just sitting in math class. There is no way love could be any more intense without actually killing a person. Besides, French-kissing somebody you don't even love really would be pretty slutty.

While she was breaking up for me, Meredith found out that Kevin wasn't grounded either. He was still coming to our party Friday night. I thought maybe we would get back together at the party. I wanted to kiss him again. I was thinking maybe it would work out better this time, but boy was I wrong.

Friday afternoon Meredith and Anne and I decorated the basement. We used a lot of crepe paper. Kids started coming over around seven-thirty and Kevin got there around eight. We ignored each other. I wasn't nervous. Plenty of time. I didn't eat anything because I wanted to keep my breath minty in case Kevin and I got back together and started to French-kiss. I went up to the kitchen at around quarter of nine to get more pretzels for the people who'd rather eat than kiss.

Mom was hovering. "There is going to be no spin the bottle in my house," she said, opening the bag for me.

"Oh, please!" I took an Altoid from Mom's tin on the counter.

Mom poured the pretzels into the bowl and flattened down the heap in the center. "Are you having fun?" she whispered.

I nodded, wondering if she was going to quiz me on why I was having fun and who I liked. I'd noticed when Kevin walked in that my mother was watching him. I wondered if she knew that it was really him I had been kissing in the hall and that it was him I liked. I wondered if she thought he was the cutest boy at the party, the best one.

"Good," she said. I could tell she was waiting for more information, but I wasn't about to hang around in the kitchen gossiping with my mother for the whole party. Is that what she wanted? Too bad. Just because I got caught kissing once at school doesn't give my mother the right to start supervising my life like I'm a ten-year-old. I was about to tell her she can trust me or not, I don't care, and that it's my life and my tongue and I can do whatever I want with both of them.

"Is Meredith?" Mom asked.

"Is Meredith what?"

"Having fun?"

"How should I know?" I asked. Meredith? What did she have to do with anything?

Mom took a breath.

Oh no, I thought. I can't handle another lecture. I will never get to the making-up-and-making-out part of the night at this rate. "Sorry," I said.

"Are you angry about something?" Mom asked. Which made me almost cry. I have no idea why.

"No!"

Mom's eyes scanned my outfit. I don't think she thought I looked very pretty. I pulled the bottom of my shirt to stretch it and said, "I just don't want to waste . . . I gotta go."

"It seems like a good party," Mom said. "Have fun."

I gritted my teeth. Sometimes lately she is so incredibly annoying. She held out the box of Altoids. I took another one, said thanks, and went back downstairs with the bowl of pretzels.

Kevin was making out with my best friend, Anne.

Her arms were around him and her tongue was in his mouth.

My wrists felt numb. I dropped the bowl of pretzels. It was plastic, so it didn't shatter; it just rolled around a little on the tiles, making whirling sounds. I meant to run upstairs, but I couldn't get my legs working. Everybody was staring at me. Well, everybody except the kissers.

Diandra started picking up pretzels and putting them back in the bowl.

When the kissing stopped, eventually, Anne saw my face and ran over to me. She dragged me to the downstairs bathroom. She thought I hated Kevin, she said. She felt terrible, especially since he was the first boy I'd ever kissed. I had to make her feel better. I told her it was no big deal.

"Are you sure?" she asked.

"Please," I said.

Then apparently she felt better because she wanted to talk about whether Kevin is a good kisser or too slobbery. She's been waiting for me to join the kissers of the world for a long time, I guess, but she's like George; she never made me feel like a loser for waiting. But apparently now that I've been kissed there is so much more to talk about.

"A little too slobbery," I said.

"You think?" Anne asked.

I shrugged. "Based on my scientific survey."

Anne laughed. She has a really wicked laugh.

"What do you think?" I managed to ask.

"I don't know," she said. "His tongue is . . ."

I stood up. I didn't want to talk about Kevin's tongue. I said I was thirsty, and Anne said so was she. We decided to get out of the bathroom and go find some sodas.

Kevin was already gone. His mother had picked him up before Anne and I opened the door. I tried to be a good host, but I was ready for everybody to go home. They didn't. I said I had a headache and went upstairs. I did have a headache, actually, but I told Mom I could handle it, please leave me alone, I am fourteen years old—I know how to cope with a headache by myself believe it or not. I got in bed and pretended to read, wondering if my sister or my best friend or at least my mother was going to come in and check on me at all. Nobody did.

I didn't go down to help clean up, despite Mom's suggestion through my closed door. Anne was sleeping over, anyway; she helped Meredith, and from their laughter I could tell they were very obviously enjoying themselves so they didn't need my assistance. At midnight they tiptoed in. I wasn't sleeping. I fell asleep when they were done whispering.

That was last weekend. This week everyone seems to think I'm either a basket case or a slut or both. I know I'm both and worse—I know I totally screwed up my first love.

It feels really weird to love someone. I think about him all the time even though Wednesday in gym he was running in this really peculiar way, all uncoordinated and doofy, his feet circling out to the sides. Even that didn't shut me down on him.

Meanwhile I asked George out. I e-mailed him. He said yes.

He's back to meeting me after each class, like he used to, and walking me to my next one. He hasn't mentioned Kevin or my new reputation. Good old George, such a gentleman.

My mother answered the phone last night and called, "Mallory, it's George!" She sounded pleased. She whispered that he's so cute. I don't know if he is or isn't. It seems beside the point.

He was calling just to say hi. We watched TV over the phone and then hung up to go get our homework done. He said he'd see me tomorrow.

"Yeah?" I asked, but he'd already hung up.

I do like George, I guess. There's nothing not to like. I feel bad for him, though. He has this idea of me that he likes a whole lot more than he'd ever like the actual, secret, horrible me. He thinks I have values and standards and morals, that I'm "mature," that I'm "deep." But I'm not the person he and my mother think I am, or at least I'm not anymore.

Because the sad truth is that I'll dump George in one hot second if Kevin ever wants me back.

ABOUT RACHEL VAIL

Rachel Vail is the award-winning author of *Wonder, Do-Over, Ever After,* and *Daring to Be Abigail.* In 1998 the first three books in her popular The Friendship Ring series and *Over the Moon,* her first picture book, were all named *Publishers Weekly* Best Books of the Year. Rachel Vail is busy at work on Mama Rex & T, her new series for young readers. Her latest picture book, *Sometimes I'm Bombaloo,* came out in spring 2002.

About her inspiration for "One Hot Second," Rachel Vail writes: "I was a bookish tenth grader loitering outside chemistry class the day before February vacation when I noticed the hottest eleventh-grade boy strutting straight toward me. He had never even said hello to me before, but there he was, staring into my eyes, reaching for my shoulders, pulling me close. A *hug,* I realized, though it was so different from a normal A-frame/pat-on-the-back hug it was almost unrecognizable to me, reeling within it. Our bodies touched all the way from our shoulders to our knees. He whispered into my hair, 'Have a good vaction,' and then walked away, leaving me wobbly for, well, about a year."

SOMEONE BOLD

SARAH DESSEN

ANGELA IS painting her nails Iced Plum and trying not to think about the heat when Samantha comes stomping down the driveway, her small face scrunched up, a fat hand wiping angrily at her eyes. It is obvious, even from a distance, that something is wrong.

"What's the matter?" Angela calls out. Samantha comes closer, up the stairs to the front porch, not speaking until she is beside Angela, waiting until she is right up close to share her anguish. Angela can see her dirty pink Keds and an ankle with a Grover Band-Aid on it out of the corner of her eye.

"They're being mean to me." Samantha tugs at her shorts, which are about two sizes too small for her. Her stomach pokes over the waistband and peeps out from beneath her T-shirt, little-kid plump.

"Who is?" Angela puts down her polish and fans her hand in the air, then reaches over and brushes Samantha's fine hair out of her eyes. It is just long enough that it pulls free and wisps around any braid or ponytail that tries to hold it back.

"Meghan and them." Samantha gestures down the road, beyond the rows of perfect lawns and houses, to a group of kids riding their bikes around the cul-de-sac. "When I came up on my bike they said, 'Look, it's the big fat dorkus,' and when I tried to catch up with them, they rode away and left me behind."

Angela bites her lip, sighing. She feels sorry for Samantha.

At nine she is just like Angela was at her age: overweight, shy, the kind of kid that gets picked last for kickball teams and eats with the teacher at lunch. Angela was that kid, and she has not forgotten even now, at eighteen, how the words of children can sting. But every day since Angela started baby-sitting for her, it has been the same story. Samantha takes off on her pink Huffy bicycle, pumping her chubby legs up the sloping driveway, only to return a few moments later in tears. Angela has run out of soothing comments and instead finds herself encouraging Samantha to go play by herself. As she thinks this, a flurry of bicycles passes across the top of the driveway; a blond girl shouts out, *"Tattletale!"* as she whizzes by, her braids swinging behind her.

"Am *not!*" Samantha shouts, stomping her foot. Angela would like to chase down that little girl, grab her, and teach her a lesson, but she knows that it is important to let Samantha fight her own battles. If she doesn't learn now, she never will. This is also something Angela knows from experience. If she'd ever fought any battle, she might be able to confront Trey about Carolyn instead of just accepting his excuses because he's the best thing she's got these days. Which is not saying much, but that's something she's trying not to think about right now.

Angela switches to the other hand. "Why don't you just go play by yourself?" she tells Samantha again. Being a baby-sitter is one quarter skill and three quarters repeating yourself, or so she's learning.

"I will," Samantha says indignantly, as if it were Angela who caused all the trouble in the first place. She bangs down the porch and up the smooth pavement to her bike, knocking at the kickstand and riding off with a slight wobble.

It has only been a month since Angela found out Trey slept with Carolyn Baker, and even though he has apologized and she has forgiven and life has gone on, something is not settling well with her. It's a nagging feeling, and a familiar one. It is as if suddenly, just in the last month, she has finally realized that she deserves better than this.

Carolyn Baker. The name makes her pop into Angela's mind, tossing her long brown hair around and laughing her snorty sorority-girl laugh. Carolyn goes to East Carolina University, drives a convertible, and is rumored to have had liposuction over Christmas when she claimed to be having her appendix out. Trey's best friend, Todd, who'd graduated a year ahead of him and Angela, was also a freshman at ECU. Trey had been going up to visit him every Saturday for at least six months before Angela's best friend, Lisa, leaned across a sticky table at Pizza Hut one night and said, "Don't you *worry* about what he might be doing there every weekend?" Up to that point it had not even dawned on Angela that Trey might like someone else. Trey, she figured, was just not that type.

Maybe it was because he was the first one she dated after she lost the weight. Just a year ago Angela had dropped forty-five pounds, a substantial chunk of the self she'd been all her life. In a way it is like losing yourself, losing weight, and after a year of measuring portions and walking two miles every day and writing down each thing she put in her mouth including gum, Angela looked up one day and saw someone else staring back at her from the mirror. Someone thin, with a tiny waist and cheekbones. Someone who could almost be described as pretty, or perky. Someone new.

But being thin and wearing all the cute little matching outfits her mother insisted on running out and buying, as if Angela had lost all the weight for her mom alone, Angela saw a different world. Men smiled at her on the street instead of averting their eyes or walking past with no acknowledgment whatsoever, as if she were a shrub or a building. She got whistles and grins, doors held open for her. It was like a secret world denied to the overweight, a magical door that only thin and pretty people slip through to a place where everything is sparkling and nice. A world of beautiful people. This is where she met Trey.

It was at a party, one she hadn't even wanted to go to, but Lisa, the party girl, had insisted. She'd even dressed Angela, in a black dress that showed her legs, then pushed her out into the crowd and promptly disappeared. Angela was standing by the door drinking way too much beer and feeling fidgety when some guy in a plaid shirt with a plastic bag on his head came over and tried to pick her up, then threw up right next to her feet. It was Trey who took her upstairs and helped her get cleaned up, then drove her home when she couldn't find Lisa anywhere. He was a gentleman that way.

He opened doors for Angela and stood up every time she entered the room, kissed her hungrily but—at least at the beginning—never pushed her to move too fast. She believed everything he told her, having no reason not to: She wasn't jaded, like Lisa, who listened to every word spoken by any man with a raised eyebrow, already doubting. Angela had never had a boyfriend before, other than a few awkward dates with the sons of her mother's friends, boys who were nice enough but looked at their watches too much, as if serving the last days of a long sentence. Even her junior-prom date was a friend of a cousin who had a favor coming. In the prom pictures his eyes are closed, a discreet space between him and Angela even though the photographer kept telling them to stand closer, stand closer.

But that had always been her problem; she couldn't stand up for herself. They dished it out and she took it, just like that, whether it be her prom date or her mother or Trey. She didn't know how to take a stand.

For instance, she'd thought it was sweet that Trey missed his friend Todd enough to drive three hours to see him every weekend. He was such a good friend, she told herself all those Friday nights she sat home alone. Now, it seemed, Angela had to face the fact that he might have been kissing Carolyn Baker hungrily in some dorm room in Greenville all those Saturdays she had sat home and watched HBO while doing her nails. And she was pretty sure that Carolyn Baker hadn't held her hands out against his chest and said quietly in the darkness that she didn't want to go that far, wasn't ready, it was too soon. She was pretty sure of that.

Because that had been the only problem she'd been aware of, at least lately. Trey wasn't happy anymore with just making out, or even going up her shirt, so she'd caved a bit, let him undo the top of her jeans. Still one night in his parents' basement he'd pushed to go further, even as she protested.

The TV was on, scattering strange shadows across their bodies: They'd been watching wrestling or something, but as she'd been distracted, the show had changed to some documentary about shipbuilding. So as Trey was whispering in her ear, saying, "Come on, come on, I promise, come on," she turned her head and saw only big schooners sailing across choppy seas, and it unnerved her. When she sat up, grabbing her purse and fumbling with her bra, Trey only sat back and sighed. No more pleading then. Nothing. Just the ships, still fighting the waves as she left, shutting the door quietly behind her.

But it hadn't been over then. Of course not. There had been a few more nights like that, a little progress made, before he'd started the trips to Greenville. She'd thought things were getting better. Really.

And she probably never would have found out about Carolyn if she hadn't showed up at his house one weekend he said he was sick to bring him some soup and crackers. He'd sounded awful on the phone, all raspy and weak, when he said he'd just see her on Monday, no don't come over, I don't want you to catch this. How considerate, she'd thought. He's thinking of my health.

Actually Trey had other things on his mind, or so Angela discovered when she knocked lightly on his door and pushed it open to find him and Carolyn in bed together. Naked. Not partially, or bra off, but full-out naked. And Angela was standing there with her thermos of soup and bag of crackers, in her cute little pink shorts outfit her mother had picked out. She didn't even see Trey's face, at least not that she remembered. She didn't look at Carolyn, either, except for the quick flash of her face as she turned it, hiding behind Trey's shoulder. All Angela could remember, actually, was the pair of red satin panties edged with black lace on the floor in front of her. And all she was thinking was that she'd never had a pair of panties like that in her life. It would never even occur to her to buy panties like that. Not in a million years.

The feeling in her stomach as she turned and walked down the stairs, slowly, with Trey calling her name behind her, was not unlike what she had felt all those days in elementary school when she stood waiting with Chester, the retarded kid, and Betty Juffers, who was hyperactive, to be picked for kickball teams. Not unlike what she had felt sitting with Mrs. Ames at lunch every day, and Mrs. Belkins and Mrs. Whitely after that. Not unlike what she felt when she saw Samantha speeding toward her on her bike, face red and shiny, running from the taunts only fat kids can hear.

Angela wipes her hair out of her eyes as she finishes her left hand, feeling her damp halter top stick to her back. Samantha is at the top of the driveway, riding in small, careful circles. The blond girl and the rest of her friends speed back by, and Samantha is momentarily hidden from view, blending in with the rest of the faces, bodies, and bicycles in Angela's sight. In a few seconds she is alone again, the sunlight glinting off the metal of her bike in little winks as her plump face, wistful and upturned, stares after them.

When Angela gets home at six o'clock, the mail has not come. This has become a real problem. She has always believed that the mail service is flawless: that the mail, even when the world is in chaos, is a regular and dependable thing, like the tides or sunrise and sunset. Not so with Angela's mailman. He is young, with a ponytail, and lopes at a snail's pace through the apartment complex where she and her mom live, stopping to rest wherever he sees fit. He has a tattoo on his forearm of a lightning bolt reaching down out of a big dark cloud. The girls in 14-B always offer him iced tea, and he sits with them on their tacky lawn furniture, his feet propped up on a planter filled with daisies, while his mail sack, with Angela's mail in it, sits beside him on the grass. Angela can see them from her kitchen window, can see the mailman as he throws his head back and gulps down tea, the girls giggling in their plastic recliners. The girls in 14-B are always coming home late, usually with men who leave very early the next morning and don't look up at Angela as she passes them in the parking lot on her way out for her walk. The girls flirt with the mailman, competing for his attention, their voices carrying over to Angela's window.

The mail arrives anywhere from nine A.M. to four-thirty P.M., or sometimes not at all, depending on how many stops the mailman makes to rest and whether the 14-B girls offer him sandwiches. This infuriates Angela. She wants to confront him, to demand her mail or his resignation, but instead she hides in the small apartment, scowling, unable to act.

She decides to call Trey: The machine picks up, his cool and gallant voice saying, "Hey, y'all, this is Trey, but I'm not here to get your call. Please leave a message and I'll get back to you as soon as I can. Have a good one," then the beep shrieking in her ear. Angela considers leaving a message, one that says all she would say if she had the nerve. Lately she has found herself looking at Trey over dinner or as he sits next to her on the couch, and she finds herself thinking ugly thoughts. It has been a month since it happened, and they've gone through the motions of forgiveness. Flowers were sent, promises made, clichés tossed around, like "It was just a stupid thing" and "She never meant anything, not like you." And Angela, faced with being alone again, caved in and accepted his apology, took him back. But it doesn't feel right; something is nagging at her. Something that wants to be set right.

When she gets his machine lately, she has a sudden urge to leave a message like, "Hello, Trey, you lying bastard. You repulse me. Have a good one." She would not leave her name. She imagines him playing it back, hearing her but not believing she could say such things. She likes to imagine the way his face would look as he wondered what she might do next.

But she has forgiven him, so instead, she hangs up when she hears the beep, saying nothing, and lies across the bed as the sun goes down, the room growing darker and cooler as it slips out of sight.

The next day Samantha is playing by herself in the driveway when the little blond girl pedals by, slowly. She is alone. She sits at the top of the driveway, her arms on the handlebars, one foot balancing the bike beneath her.

Angela sees her watching Samantha, who is busy trying to dress her Ken doll. Ken is not cooperating; his head pops off every time she tries to pull his plaid sweater over it. Barbie is lying naked nearby, waiting for her evening gown.

"Hey," the little blond girl says.

Samantha looks up. "What?"

"Whatcha doin'?"

"Playing Barbies." Samantha hesitates, holding Ken's head in her fist. "Want to play?"

Angela puts down her book. The little blond girl seems about to say yes when a group of kids on their bikes appears at the top of the driveway. They gather around and look down at Samantha, and Angela can already tell what will happen.

"Hey, Meghan! What are you doing? Gonna play with the big fat dorkus?" The boy laughs and the blond girl turns red; in a moment the kids have all disappeared, riding at full speed down the sidewalk.

The blond girl scowls at Samantha. "I wouldn't play with you if you were the last big fat dorkus on earth. Barbies! Only babies play Barbies." She pedals away while Samantha sits on the pavement, Ken's head squeezed tightly in her fist. She looks over, so sweet and sad there on the pavement, her hair back in pink elephant barrettes and her Barbie suitcase beside her, its contents sorted neatly into evening and casual wear, but this time she doesn't say anything. She puts Ken's head back on and reaches for Barbie, holding her around her tiny waist.

She's accepting it, Angela realizes, and it bothers her more than she thought it would. She wants to chase after that little blond girl and grab her by her shoulders, to say something forceful and real, all the things that at nine and ten and eleven she held in and no one said for her. But she doesn't. She takes Samantha inside and they drink Kool-Aid in the breakfast nook until her parents come home. Then Angela drives back through town to her apartment and her empty mailbox and blames the mailman for everything.

Sometimes she dreams she's fat again, or on her way to fat. She's always eating in these dreams, usually ice cream or big fudgy brownies, one right after another. And then, right as she's stuffing another spoonful or handful into her mouth, she has a realization: the weight. It's coming back. And then suddenly she's growing, her clothes tightening, all the little pink and white and yellow shorts sets bursting at their seams as she tries to hold them together, tries to stop it all from happening, but in vain. She always wakes up hot and flustered, her hands immediately spreading to her thighs and stomach, feeling the tight skin and muscle, reassuring.

The days are hot—hotter, it seems, than any other summer. She and Samantha take refuge at the neighborhood pool, where her fingers turn prunish and blue and her skin a deep brown. Trey takes a trip to Greenville and doesn't call. And the dreams keep coming, more and more frequently. Soon it is all she thinks of as she sleeps, and she knows it must mean something.

It is the hottest day on record when it happens. She and Samantha are in the kitchen eating Rice Krispies Treats and playing Risk and suddenly Angela has this feeling. A gut feeling, and something in it is telling her to call Trey. Right then. That it's important, more important than Samantha working her armies across Asia and all of Angela's strongholds.

"But we're playing," Samantha whines as Angela starts dialing. "And I'm winning. It's your roll."

"Hold on," Angela says. "Have another Rice Krispie Treat."

She can tell something is up just by the way he says hello. It's the same way you can always tell when someone is just faking walking out a door, letting it fall shut and standing there out of sight to see what you'll do when you think they're gone. Trey is up to something. Angela has a flash of those red satin panties with black lace edging. And she knows. Instantly, she knows.

"Listen," Trey says in his lazy drawl, "I'm busy. I'll call you back."

"No," Angela says. She doesn't sound like herself. A voice is muffled in the background, his hand against the receiver, covering up. She's there. Angela can feel her. And suddenly she wants to hang up, to take him at his word and believe, like she wanted to believe it could just be forgotten, just one mistake, meaning nothing. After all, she has never been the kind of girl who expects much: a cute boyfriend with a winning smile, one who opens doors for her, must come with some kind of compromise. But she's not so sure she believes that anymore.

Samantha has gone on playing without her, a Rice Krispies Treat clamped in her hand. She is rolling the dice, moving her forces to take over the world. With each throw she spreads farther across countries, crossing borders and toppling empires. She is smiling.

"Come on, Angela," she whispers. Angela is still holding the phone, listening to Trey cover the receiver with his palm, hearing a voice beyond that, knowing that he's sure she will leave it at this and not question him. In his own way Trey is like all those taunting kids on the bikes who pedaled madly through her childhood, and now Samantha's—he thinks he has the key to her. Thinks that with one word, or one sentence, or just the right phrase, he can turn any lock she bars against him, any army she puts in place to guard her borders and strengthen her offensive. He will always have the lucky roll, or so he thinks. She's like a formula that's been tested again and again, with only the variable changing each time.

"No?" Trey says, repeating her, then laughs softly. He thinks she's kidding. "Come on, honey. That's not like you."

Samantha is still rolling, jiggling the dice. Her armies have spread even farther. She holds the balance of the world in one sticky hand.

"You don't know me," Angela says to Trey. She isn't that sure she even knows herself, or her new self, free of forty-five pounds and a fat kid's smile, free of her mother's shorts-and-shirt sets, and capable of changing everything, of having a lucky roll herself. Maybe it's time, she thinks, time to change those boundaries, to push back those borders. To claim a new country under a new name.

But she doesn't tell any of this to Trey. She leaves him wondering at the other end of the line, laughing his easy laugh as she hangs up on him and lets Samantha rule the world, holding her chubby arms over her head, the victor.

The mailman's truck is parked at the front of the complex when Angela pulls into her parking space. She has not gotten her mail. As she gets a glass of water in her kitchen, she can see the mailman on the 14-B terrace: He is eating what looks like chips and dip. She stands in some sort of trance, watching him for almost thirty minutes. The sun is beginning to set behind the trees in her backyard; a bunch of little kids in neon bathing suits pass beneath her window on their way to the pool. One of them is wearing sunglasses.

Angela watches as the mailman accepts another glass of tea from the louder of the two 14-B girls. He stretches his legs out in front of him, his regulation mail-carrier shorts smoothed across his legs, the mail sack lying beneath his chair.

She can't say what comes over her. But soon Angela pushes open her back door and finds herself walking briskly through the grass toward the girls' terrace, across several backyards, the water from a sprinkler misting her face. She comes up behind the mailman's plastic recliner, surprising one of the girls, who sits dumbfounded, holding her iced-tea glass and a chip heaped with dip in midair.

"Excuse me." Angela says this loudly, sounding like someone else, someone bold. The mailman turns around and grins at her. His stupid ponytail curls over his collar. It is very quiet except for the gleeful shrieking of children from the pool; someone is yelling "Marco!" every few seconds.

Angela takes a deep breath. The mailman is still grinning at her. She knows she is not smiling. "I want my mail," she says. Then, because she's already gone so far, she adds, "Now."

The mailman is no longer smiling. She pulls up the sack: The mailman tries to protest and spills his tea across his uniform top, drenching his front pocket in a deep brown. Angela digs her hands through the mail, through heaps of catalogs and envelopes, names all running together; she's sure she'll never find her own, but then suddenly, as if fate has given it to her, it's in her hand. She pulls it out and clutches it against her chest, the victor. The mailman is covered in iced tea; the girls are rushing around with towels, looking nervous.

The mailman is flustered. "Hey, you can't do that. You just can't do that." He is trying to organize his sack while one girl dabs at him with towels.

"Yes," Angela says, "I can." Then she pauses before adding, "Have a good one."

Walking back to her own yard, she thinks that's what it must come down to: little victories, small steps that gather momentum and run faster and faster together, growing in size and shape. Maybe it begins with mailmen and can go any-where from there. She's not sure what will come next. She can only think of all that unexplored territory waiting to be conquered.

Angela goes to the pool and dips her feet into the cool wa-ter, her mail lying on the pavement beside her. The kids are bobbing through the blue water, their calling voices carrying across the pool and over Angela's head and rising above her into the trees. They take turns diving to the bottom, their out-lines wavy beneath the ripples made by Angela's feet. Then one by one they shoot to the surface, their faces bursting with a splash into the moist summer air.

ABOUT SARAH DESSEN

Sarah Dessen grew up in Chapel Hill, North Carolina, where she also attended college at the University of North Carolina. Her first novel, *That Summer,* was published in 1996 and named an ALA Best Book for Young Adults. She is also the author of *Someone Like You* and *Keeping the Moon,* both ALA Quick Picks for Young Adults and *School Library Journal* Best Books of the Year, and *Dreamland,* another ALA Best Book for Young Adults. Her fifth novel for young adults will be published in 2002.

About desire Sarah Dessen writes, "In seventh grade, there was a guy who I was completely in love with. We shared one class, where I'd stare at him unabashedly for fifty minutes every day, wishing he would look at me. Then, late one Friday night, my phone rang. It was him! I almost died. I was so excited . . . until he asked if I thought my best friend liked him. I was crushingly depressed. I think this sort of thing happens to everyone at least once, but the first time is always the worst."

LORENA

JACQUELINE WOODSON

THERE IS a building I used to know. One evening the sun dipped down bright pink and disappeared. *Magic*, Lorena whispered, her lips touching my ear. *That sun. You. Us. Everything. Amazing.* Amazing the way everything is when you're fifteen. I was fifteen. Lorena was fifteen and a half. Older than me in so many other ways too. Her hair was black and curly and wild. There was a beauty mark beside her nose. Later, up close, I would see that it was heart-shaped, a tiny black heart on a light brown face.

Black or white? kids at school would ask.
Neither and both, Lorena would say. *Which one do you need me to be?*

Lorena. Lorena. Your name never goes away from me.

A fire took the building soon after that sunset. My mother writes to me: *The city's tearing that building down. The one your friend used to live in. It's just a skeleton now anyway.*

Fire does that—leaves skeletons.

* * *

That building—the one the sun set behind? Lorena died there. It's a long story. No—it's a short story. The memories around it like petals—she loves me, she loves me not; she lives, she lives not. She loved me.

Summer left. Fall came. Then winter, cold and bleak and gray and long. Then after that, the *dead* of winter—no afternoon, just late morning and then night. I turned sixteen. I grew two inches taller. My hair grew out, wiry and wild. Some days I slept and slept. Some nights I wandered the streets, heading nowhere. My throat hollowed out. Dark circles appeared beneath my eyes. My hands shook some mornings. My heart broke into a million pieces of glass inside my chest. Once I walked to the park in the middle of the night and screamed. Lorena had been dead a long time by then.

They say. They say. They say:

> *She's not coming back.*
> *New home.*
> *Your mind's older than your years.*
> *Sleep now.*
> *Wake up.*
> *Where'd you go?*
> *We want Natalie back.*
> *Natalie. Natalie.*
> *Earth calling Natalie.*
> *Slow down.*
> *Come back.*
> *Put it behind you.*

Move on.
Stay awhile.
Eat something.
Rest now.

Some days I believe Lorena's still in that building—her back pressed into a corner, light coming through the window and into her eyes. The sun sinking. Bright pink. Deep blue. Then gone. Me moving toward her. Slowly. Lorena throwing her head back and laughing, whispering, *Silly, silly Natalie. God, how I love you, girl.* Her hands, everywhere at once. And me falling. Falling.

*   *   *

I would like to say it was fire that took my first love. *Smoke inhalation*, I would say. *She never knew*, I would say. *The flames, they never even reached her.*

*   *   *

People knew us. People loved us. People hated us. They said, *You two are so cute together.* They asked, *What do two girls do?* They said, *I had a friend like that but she was still cool.* They said, *But you're both so pretty, why can't you get boyfriends?* They whispered, they laughed. Sometimes they called us names. Sometimes they called us sexy. They said we were brave. They said we were crazy.

*   *   *

My mother takes a long drag from her cigarette, looks at me through half-closed eyes. We are in the kitchen. Behind her there is a window. Two little kids are jumping rope in front of our gate, behind my mother. Behind the thin stream of smoke.

"Look at your hair now," my mother says. "You used to be so damn beautiful I could hardly believe you were a part of me."

"I was never a part of you."

"Yes, Natalie." She takes another drag, lets the smoke out slowly. "Once you were."

Sixteen moves on like this—slowly. My mother and I becoming strangers, other sixteen-year-olds seeming young and dumb. The building, a shell with my memory of Lorena still inside. They say, *Move on, Natalie. You of the pretty bones.* They say, *Model, act, sing.* They say, *Be fabulous,* then laugh. Their laughter rises up out of them. Easily. Nothing choking it back. Strangers. They become strangers. They say, *Let her go. After all, she was only in your life for a short time.* They say. They say.

Then I am sixteen and a half, on a bus heading to a school in New England. Outside the bus window, leaves are gold and red and green—bright like I've never seen leaves before. *Concord next stop,* the driver says. I pull my duffel from the rack above me. She is with me still.

Who do you call when she doesn't show for school? Days pass, the knock on her door unanswered. Standing in her hallway, you scream her name. Lorena. Again and again and again. Lorena. Lorena. Lorena. Your heart is breaking. Who do you call? How alone you are. How utterly alone you are.

* * *

I want to tell you this—that it does not hurt when the news comes. The phone pressed too hard against your ear, the words coming quietly between breaths—*I'm sorry*, the caller says. And even though the phone's trying to find its way inside your head, trying to press itself past your ear into your skull, the words stop outside your brain somewhere. Just float in some empty pool of blood and whatever else lives in that space between skin and skull and brain.

"Why are you apologizing? You didn't do anything." And your voice is not your own anymore. Won't ever be again.

"Natalie, are you all right?"

That's your mother calling as she hears your feet heavy and fast on the stairs, hears the door to your room slamming hard. She doesn't see the sun from your window like you do. Doesn't know how much it hurts to watch it sink down like that. Like nothing has changed at all.

And lying there, with your mother's voice calling up, *Natalie? Natalie? Are you all right?* and behind her voice, the one still floating around in your head. *I'm sorry . . .* , what you remember is the first time. Your mind just takes you there—a defense mechanism maybe, like the way you duck when you see a thing coming at you out of the corner of your eye—before you focus on it, you move—just in case.

So you duck beneath your covers, pull the comforter up over your head, and make believe it never happened. Nothing ever happened to you.

* * *

Some days I can leave my body and watch it from afar.

* * *

Here is what death does. It takes away everywhere—a little bit of your mind here, somebody else's smile there, the quiet beauty of cappuccino with lots of foam in an East Side café. It takes away perfect moments. Makes what was so awesome painful to remember. Like Lorena's eyes.

The first time she looked at me— geometry, third period, right before art and right after second-period gym—which is the stupidest time of day to have gym because who is awake enough to run at nine-thirty in the morning? That was a long time ago. She was the new girl—just moved here from Indiana, a state I'd never given a second thought to until the word came from her—*Indiana*—soft and slow as a song. And her eyes slanting down a little at the corners when she smiled and always. Just a little. Just enough for me to see those eyes everywhere after that first day.

"Why?"

"Why what?"

"Why'd your family move from Indiana to New York?"

"Not everybody. Just me alone."

"You're lying. In tenth grade?"

"I don't lie." Her face serious suddenly. Her eyes almost mean.

"But how?"

"All it takes is money and some signatures. And I've got a ton of pens."

The way my heart dropped when she looked at me and smiled. The way gym crawled by and geometry didn't. The way her hair smelled—like jasmine and heat and something metallic, unfamiliar.

"You're a dyke too, aren't you, Natalie?"

"A what?"

It was raining outside our geometry window—hard, heavy drops. It was winter and the classroom was cold. I shivered. Moved an inch closer to her.

"You like girls, don't you?"

"I like *you*."

"I know. I know you do. I saw it that first day. Right there, in those pretty brown eyes." Indiana slipping around her words, softening them, slowing them down.

Then her hand on my thigh, warmer than anything I'd ever felt before. Softer, too. "What does it mean, then?"

Lorena smiled and winked at me. "It's means we're from the same family. Midnight's Children. That's what I read once. People who like people like themselves can only come out after midnight."

"When it's safe?"

"It's never safe."

That smile again. And the hand, a little higher on my thigh. And squeezing.

* * *

It is her mother who calls you. All the way here from Indiana and never even been to New York before. She is only a voice on the phone.

"Your number was written in her notebook. You were her friend, weren't you?"

"Yes, ma'am."

"Did you know she was using. . . . Did you know she was an addict? Are you an addict too? Didyoukillmy Lorenagiveherthedrugstheysaysheoverdosedwasityouwasityouwasityou—"

The phone slipping away from your ear slowly . . .

"Oh God, my sweet daughter. My Lorena."

Oh God, my sweet Lorena.

                          *   *   *

You came here without your parents?

 They didn't want to come.

 Are you scared?

 *Always. Never. Always. Never. Kiss me, Natalie. When you
kiss me, I'm not scared of anything.*

                          *   *   *

The school is bigger than in the pictures. There are kids everywhere. And parents kissing them on the foreheads and cheeks.
Tearing up as they wave good-bye. Pressing money into their
hands. *Call me,* they yell. *Write,* they say. *Eat.*

 Dexter Academy. Where Fine Young Men and Women Begin.

 My duffel is heavy on my shoulder. I feel a long, long way
from home.

                          *   *   *

Five small scabs by her toes first. *Mosquito bites,* she said. But
in the light I see that her feet are covered with tiny raised
scars. And then later, a syringe bent near the trash can. *Are
you a diabetic?* And Lorena, with those eyes slanting down,
pressed her hand against my chin and smiled. *Oh, Natalie, Natalie, Natalie. My sweet baby girl.*

Her apartment, a small studio on the ninth floor. Brooklyn
Bridge in the distance. And from another window the Statue
of Liberty, all the way over there. When the wind blew hard in
the winter, the building swayed and Lorena and I lay on her

futon and laughed, scared and excited all at once. Sometimes I spent the night. In the darkness I'd whisper, *This is everything, Lorena.*

And pressing her face into my neck, Lorena nodded.

Like it would always be so.

In the mornings, walking around her tiny apartment naked, I felt grown-up. And free. And so, so sure.

*　*　*

"I'd like to meet this new friend's parents," my mother said.

"Yeah. Whatever."

*　*　*

Do you ever want to disappear, Natalie?

No. Not really.

What magic do you want, then? Everybody wants some magic.

To be everywhere at one time. Invisible sometimes. But not always. What do you want?

I want to step out of my body. I want to see who I am from a distance.

That's strange, Lorena.

I know how to do it.

*　*　*

You never ask what you don't want to know.

*　*　*

Dexter Academy. Where Fine Young Men and Women Begin.

Again.

*　*　*

Start from the beginning. There was a building once. And inside lived a girl named Lorena. The edges of her eyes tilted down. You've seen people like this. Maybe you've even loved them.

Start at the beginning again. Dexter Academy. I am seventeen. In physics class the first day, there is a girl who looks at me and smiles. *Sit here*, her smile says. *I think we have something in common.*

I am seventeen years old. My name is Natalie. Before I fall in love this time, I will check for scars.

About Jacqueline Woodson

Jacqueline Woodson is the author of several award-winning novels, including *I Hadn't Meant to Tell You This* and *From the Notebooks of Melanin Sun* (both Coretta Scott King Honor Books and ALA Best Books for Young Adults), *If You Come Softly*, *The House You Pass on the Way*, and *Lena*. Her novel *Miracle's Boys* won the 2000 Coretta Scott King Award and the *Los Angeles Times* Book Prize. She lives in Brooklyn, New York.

"The first time I fell in love," Jacqueline Woodson recalls, "I was ten and the object of my affection was my fifth-grade teacher, Ms. Vivo. I remember the day my belt broke. It was one of those hip seventies plastic belts with flowers painted on it. I was wearing it with a pair of hip huggers that were a bit too big and a bodysuit that was a tad too tight. Ms. Vivo, stapler in hand, rescued me, giving me a sidelong smile as she stapled the belt together. As the class gathered around her, watching her work, someone said, 'You fix things better than my dad,' and Ms. Vivo laughed and said, 'Well, I'm a feminist.' Although I didn't know what a feminist was, I knew I wanted to be one too. I wanted to fix things and have a sidelong smile that made hearts go crazy. And teach. And learn. And be free."

TEAM MEN

EMMA DONOGHUE

THAT WAS the kindest thing Saul could say about anyone, that he was a real team man.

"Jonathan," he used to tell his son over their bacon, eggs, sausage, and beans, "a striker's not put up front for personal glory. You'll only end up a star player for Yorkshire if you keep your mind on playing for the good of the team. Them as tries to be first shall be last and vice versa."

Jon just kept on eating his toast.

Saul King believed in fuel first thing in the morning, when there was plenty of time ahead to burn it up. "Breakfast like a legend, dine like a journeyman, and sup like a sub." That made him cackle with laughter.

The boy was just sixteen and nearly six feet tall. Headers were his strong point. When the ball sailed down to him, he could feel his neck tighten and every bit of force in his body surge toward the hard plate at the front of his skull. The crucial thing was to be ready for the ball, to meet all its force and slam it back into the sky. On good days Jon felt hard and shiny as a mirror. He knew that if Mars came falling down, he could meet it head-on and rocket it into the next galaxy.

But by now he had learned to pay no attention to his dad before a game. If Jon let the warnings get to him, he couldn't swallow. If he didn't eat enough, he found himself knackered at halftime. If he flagged, he missed passes, and the goalmouth seemed ten miles away. If the team lost, his dad took it personally, and harder than a coach should. Once when Jon fluffed a penalty kick, Saul didn't speak a word to him for a week.

"Nerves of steel," the graying man said finally as they sat at opposite ends of the table, waiting for Mum to bring a fresh pot of tea.

Jon's fork clinked against his plate. "What's that, Dad?"

"If a striker hasn't got nerves of steel when they're needed, he's no right to take a penalty kick at all."

His son listened and learned. As if he had a choice.

The lads were already having a kickabout on the field when the Kings drove up. Saul got out and watched the lads over his shoulder. "Well, well," he said, "who have we here?"

One unfamiliar coppery head, breaking away from the pack. "Oh yeah, Shaq said he might bring someone from school," Jon mentioned, hauling his bag out of the backseat.

"Now there's a pair of legs," breathed Saul. He and his son stood a foot apart, watching the new boy run. He was runt-sized but he moved as sleekly as cream.

"A winger?" hazarded Jon.

"We'll see," said Saul, mysterious.

Davy turned out to be seventeen. Up close he didn't look so short; his limbs were narrow but pure muscle. The youngest of eight, one of those big, rackety Irish families. His face went red as strawberries when he ran, but he never seemed to get out of breath; his laugh got a bit hoarser, that was all. Beside him Jon felt lumbering and huge.

In the dressing room after that first practice, Davy played his guitar as if it were electric. He sang along, confidently raucous.

> *"I get knocked down*
> *But I get up again. . . ."*

"Best put a bit of meat on those bones," observed Saul, and loaded Davy down with five bags of high-protein supplement. It turned out Davy lived just down the road from the Kings, so Saul insisted on giving him a lift home.

After a fortnight Davy was pronounced a real team man. He was to be the new striker. Jon was switched to midfield. "It's not a demotion," his father repeated. "This is a team, not a bloody corporation."

Jon looked out the car window and thought about playing on a team where the coach wouldn't be his dad, wouldn't shove him from one position to another just to prove a point about not giving his son any special treatment. Jon visualized himself becoming a legend in some sport Saul King had never tried, could hardly spell, even: badminton maybe, or curling, or luge. The thing was, all he'd ever wanted to play was soccer.

Jon was over the worst of his sulks by the next training session. He had every reason to hate this Davy, but it didn't happen. The boy was a born striker, Jon had to admit; it would have been nonsense to put him anywhere else on the field. He wasn't a great header, but he was magic with his feet. And midfield had its own satisfactions, Jon found.

"You lot are the big cog in the team's engine," Saul told the midfielders solemnly. "You slack off for a second, the game will fall apart."

Pounding along with the ball at his feet, Jon saw Davy out of the corner of his eye. "With ya!" Jon passed the ball sideways, and Davy took it without even looking. Only after he'd scored did he spin round to give Jon his grin.

"Your dad's a laugh. I mean," Davy corrected himself, "he's all right. He knows a lot."

"Not half as much as he thinks," said Jon, soaping his armpits.

"Is it true what Shaq says about him, that he got to the semi-final of the 1979 Football Association Cup?"

Jon nodded, sheepish.

Davy, under the stream of water, sprayed like a whale. "Wow. What did he play?"

"Keeper." On impulse Jon stepped closer to Davy's ear. "Dad'd flay me if he knew I told you this. He's never forgiven himself."

"What? What?" The boy's eyes were very green.

"He flapped at it. The winning goal."

Davy sucked his breath in. It made a clean musical note.

In October the days shortened. One foul wet afternoon Saul made them run fifteen laps of the field before they even started, and by the time he finally blew the whistle, they had mud to their waists and it was too dark to see the ball. Naz tripped over Jon's foot and landed on his elbow. "You big ape," moaned Naz. "You lanky ape-man."

The other lads thought this was very funny.

"You can't let them get to you," Davy said casually afterward while they were warming down.

"Who?" said Jon, as if from a million miles away.

Davy shrugged. "Any of them. Anyone who calls you names."

Jon chewed his lip.

"I've got five big brothers," Davy added when he and Jon were sitting in the back of the car counting their bruises. "And my sisters are even worse. They've always taken the mickey out of me. One of them called me the Little Stain till she got married."

A grin loosened Jon's jaw. He stared out the window at his father, who was collecting the training cones.

"Just ignore the lads and remember what a good player you are."

"Maybe I'm not," said Jon, looking down into Davy's red hair.

"Maybe you're *what?*" Davy let out a yelp of laughter. "Jon-boy, you're the best. You've got a perfect soccer brain, and you're a sweet crosser of the ball."

Jon was glad of the twilight then. Blood sang in his cheeks.

Davy came round every couple of days now. Mrs. King often asked him to stop for dinner. "That boy's not getting enough at home," she observed darkly.

But Jon thought Davy looked all right as he was.

Jon's little sister, Michaela, sat beside Davy at the table whenever she got the chance, even if she did call him Short Arse. She was only fifteen but she looked old enough. As she was always reminding Jon, girls matured two years faster.

Davy ended up bringing Michaela to the local Halloween club night, and Jon brought her friend Tasmin. While the girls were on line for chips, Davy followed Jon into the loos. Afterward Jon could never be sure who'd started messing around; it just happened. It was sort of a joke and sort of a dare. In a white stall with a long crack in the wall, they unzipped their jeans. They kept looking down; they didn't meet each other's eyes.

It was over in two minutes. It took longer to stop laughing.

When they got back to the girls, the chips were gone cold

and Michaela wanted to know what was so funny. Jon couldn't think of anything, but Davy said it was just an old Diana joke. Tasmin said in that case they could keep it to themselves because she didn't think it was very nice to muck around with the dead.

After Halloween some people said Davy was going out with Michaela. Jon didn't know what that meant, exactly. He didn't think Davy and Michaela did stuff together, anyway. He didn't know what to think.

Saul King expressed no opinion on the matter. But he'd started laying into Davy at practice. "Mind your back! Mind your house!" he bawled, hoarse. "Keep them under pressure!"

Davy said nothing, just bounced around, grinning as usual.

"Where's your bleeding eyes?"

"Somebody's not the golden boy anymore," Peter remarked to Naz under his breath.

Saul said he had errands to do in town, so Jon and Davy could walk home for once.

"Your dad's being a bit of an arse these days," commented Davy as they turned the first corner.

"Don't call him that," said Jon.

"But he is one."

Jon shook his heavy head. "Don't call him my dad, I mean."

"Oh."

The silence stretched between them. "It's like the honey jar," said Jon.

Davy glanced up. His lashes were like a cat's.

"I was about three, right, and I wanted a bit of honey from the jar, but he said no. He didn't put the jar away or anything, just said no and left it sitting there about six inches in front of me. So the minute he was out of the room I opened it up and stuck my spoon in, of course. And I swear he must have been waiting because he was in and had that spoon snatched out of my hand before it got near my face."

"What's wrong with honey?" asked Davy, bewildered.

"Nothing."

"I thought it was good for you."

"It wasn't anything to do with the honey," said Jon, dry-throated. "He just wanted to win."

Davy walked beside him, mulling it over.

They went the long way, through the park. When they passed a gigantic yew tree, Davy turned his head to Jon and grinned like a shark.

Without needing to say a word, they ducked and crawled underneath the tree. The dark branches hung down around them like curtains. Nobody could have seen what they were up to; a passerby wouldn't even have known they were there. Jon forgot to be embarrassed. He did a sliding tackle on Davy and toppled him onto the soft damp ground. "Man on!" yelped

Davy, pretending to be afraid. They weren't cold anymore. They moved with sleek grace this time. It was telepathic. It was perfect timing.

"For Christ's sake, stay onside," Saul bawled at his team.

Davy's sneakers blurred; he moved like the legendary Maradona, Jon thought. The boy darted round the field confusing the defenders, playing to the imaginary crowd.

"Don't bother trying to impress us with the fancy footwork, Irish," screamed Saul into the wintry wind, "just try kicking the ball. This is footie, not bloody Riverdance."

Afterward in the showers Jon watched the hard curve of Davy's shoulder. He wanted to touch it, but Naz was three feet away. He took a surreptitious glance at his friend's face, but it was shrouded in steam.

Saul never gave Jon and Davy a lift home from practice anymore. He said the walk was good exercise and Lord knew they could do with it.

"I don't know why, but your dad is out to shaft me," said Davy on the long walk home.

"No he's not," said Jon weakly.

"Is so. He said he thought I might make less of a fool of myself in defense."

"Defense?" repeated Jon, shrill. "That's bollocks. Last Saturday's match, you scored our only goal."

"You set it up for me. Saul said only a paraplegic could have missed it."

Jon tried to remember the shot. He couldn't tell who'd done what. On a good day he and Davy moved like one player, thought the same thing at the same split second.

"I don't suppose there's any chance he knows about us?"

Jon was so shocked he stopped walking. He had to put his hand on the nearest wall or he'd have fallen. The stones were cold against his fingers. Us, he thought. There was an us. An us his dad might know about.

"No way," he said at last, hoarsely.

Jon knew there were rules, even if they'd never spelled them out. He and Davy were sort of mates and sort of something else. They didn't waste time talking about it. In one way it was like soccer—the sweaty tussle of it, the heart-pounding thrill—and in another way, it was like a game played on Mars, with unwritten rules and different gravity.

The afternoons were getting colder. On Bonfire Night they took the risk and did it in Jon's room. The door had no lock. They kept the stereo turned up very loud so there wouldn't be any suspicious silences. Outside the fireworks went off at intervals like bombs. Jon's head pounded with noise and terror. It was the best time yet.

Afterward, when they were slumped in opposite corners of

the room looking like two ordinary postmatch players, Jon turned down the music. Davy said out of nowhere, "I was thinking of telling the folks."

"Telling them what?" asked Jon before thinking. Then he understood, and his stomach furled into a knot.

"You know. What I'm like." Davy let out a mad chuckle.

"You're not . . ." His voice trailed off.

"I am, you know." Davy still sounded as if he were talking about the weather. "I've had my suspicions for years. I thought I'd give it a try with your sister, but *nada*, to be honest."

Jon thought he was going to throw up. "Would you tell them about us?"

"Only about me," Davy corrected him. "Name no names and all that."

"You never would."

"I'll have to sometime, won't I?"

"Why?" asked Jon, choking.

"Because it's making me nervous," explained Davy lightly, "and I don't play well when I'm nervous. I know my family are going to freak out of their tiny minds whenever I tell them, so I might as well get it over with."

He was brave, Jon thought. But he had to be stopped. "Listen, you mad moron," said Jon fiercely, "you can't tell anyone."

Davy sat up and straightened his shoulders. He looked small but not at all young; his face was an adult's. "Is that meant to be an order? You sound like your dad," he added with a hint of mockery.

"He'll know," whispered Jon. "Your parents'll guess it's me. They'll tell my dad."

"They won't. They'll be too busy beating the tar out of me."

"My dad's going to find out."

"How will he?" said Davy reasonably.

"He—he just will," stammered Jon. "He'll kill me. He'll get me by the throat and never let go."

"Bollocks," said Davy too lightly. "We're not kids anymore. The sky's not going to fall in on us. You're just freaking out at the thought of anyone calling you a faggot, aren't you?"

"Don't say that."

"It's only a word. Get used to it."

"We're not, anyway," he told Davy coldly. "That's not what we are."

The boy's mouth crinkled with amusement. "Oh, so what are we then?"

"We're mates," said Jon through a clenched throat.

One coppery eyebrow went up.

"Mates who mess around a bit."

"*Fag-got! Fag-got!*" Davy sang the words quietly.

Jon's hand shot out to the stereo and turned it way up to drown him out. Next door Michaela started banging on the wall. "Jonathan!" she wailed. He turned it down a little but kept his hand on the knob.

"Get out," he said.

Davy stared back at him blankly. Then he reached for his jacket and got up in one fluid movement. He looked like a scornful god. He looked as if nothing could ever knock him down.

Jon avoided Davy all week. He walked home from the training sessions while Davy was still in the shower. In the back of his mind he was preparing a contingency plan. Deny everything. Laugh. Say the sick pervert made it all up.

Nobody else seemed to notice the two friends weren't on speaking terms. Everyone was preoccupied with the big match on Saturday. At night Jon gripped himself like a drowning man clinging to a spar.

Saturday came at last. The field was muddy and badly cut up before they even started. The other team were thugs, especially an enormous winger with a mustache. From the kickoff Saul's team played worse than they ever had before. The left back crashed into his central defender, whose nose bled all down his shirt. Jon moved as if he were shackled. Whenever he had to pass the ball to Davy, it fell short or went wide by a mile. It was as if there were a shield around the red-haired boy and nothing could get through. Davy was caught offside three times in the first half. Then when Jon pitched up a loose ball on the edge of his own penalty area, one of the other team's forwards bigtoed a fluke shot into the top right-hand corner.

"You're running round like blind men," Saul told his team at halftime with sorrow and contempt.

By the start of the second half, the rain was falling unremittingly. The fat winger stood on Peter's foot, and the ref never saw a thing. "Look," bawled Peter, trying to pull his shoe off to show the marks of the cleats.

The other team found this hilarious. "Wankers!" "Faggots!" crowed the fat boy.

Rage fired up Jon's thudding heart, stoked his muscles. He would have liked to take the winger by the throat and press his thumbs in till they met vertebrae. What was it Saul always used to tell him? No son of mine gets himself sent off for temper. Jon made himself turn and jog away. No son of mine, said the voice in his head.

Naz chipped the ball high over the defense. Jon was there first, poising himself under the flight of the ball. It was going to be a beautiful header. It might even turn the match around.

"Davy's," barked Davy, jogging backward toward Jon.

Jon kept his eyes glued to the falling ball. "Jon's."

"It's mine!" Davy repeated at his elbow, crowding him.

"Sod off!" He didn't look. He shouldered Davy away, harder than he meant to. Then all of a sudden Jon knew how it was going to go. He wasn't ready to meet the ball; he didn't believe he could do it. He lost his balance, and the ball came down on the side of his head and crushed him into the mud.

*　*　*

Jon had whiplash.

Saul came home from the next training session and said Davy was off the team.

"You bastard!" said Jon.

His father stared, slack-jawed. Michaela's fork froze halfway to her mouth. "Jonathan!" appealed their mother.

Above his foam whiplash collar, Jon could feel his face burn. But he opened his mouth and it all spilled out. "You're not a coach, you're a drill sergeant. You picked Davy to bully because you knew he's going to be a better player than you ever were. And now you've kicked him off the team just to prove you can. So much for team bloody spirit!"

"Jonathan." His father's face was dark, unreadable. "It was the lad who dropped out. He's quit the team and he's not coming back."

One afternoon at the end of a fortnight, Davy came round. Jon was on his own in the living room, watching an old France '98 video of England versus Argentina. He thought Davy looked different: baggy-eyed, older somehow.

Davy stared at the television. "Has Owen scored yet?"

"Ages ago. They're nearly at penalties." Jon kept his eyes on the screen.

Davy dropped his bag by the sofa but didn't sit down, didn't take his jacket off. In silence they watched the agonizing shoot-out.

When it was over, Jon hit rewind. "If Beckham hadn't got himself sent off, we'd have demolished them," he remarked.

"In your dreams," said Davy. They watched the flickering figures. After a long minute he added, "I've been meaning to come round, actually, to say, you know, sorry and all that."

"It's nothing much, just a bit of whiplash," said Jon, deliberately obtuse. He put his hand to his neck, but his fingers were blocked by the foam collar.

"You'll get over it. No bother."

"Yeah," said Jon bleakly. "So," he added, not looking at Davy, "did you talk to your parents?"

"Yeah." The syllable was flat. "Don't worry, your name didn't come up."

"I didn't—"

"Forget it," interrupted Davy softly. He was staring at the video as it rewound: a green square covered in little frenzied figures who ran backward, fleeing from the ball.

That subject seemed closed.

"I hear you're not playing these days," said Jon.

"That's right," said Davy more briskly. "Thought I should get down to the books for a while, before my A levels."

Jon stared at him.

"I'm off to college next September, touch wood." Davy

rapped on the coffee table. "I've already got an offer of a place in law at Lancaster, but I'll need two B's and an A."

Law? Jon nodded, then winced as his neck twinged. So much he'd never known about Davy, never thought to ask. "You could sign up again in the summer, though, after your exams, couldn't you?" he asked as neutrally as he could.

There was a long pause before Davy shook his head. "I don't think so, Jon-boy."

So that was it, Jon registered. Not a proper ending. More like a match called off because of a hailstorm, or because the star player just walked off the field.

"I mean, I'll miss it, but when it comes down to it, it's only a game, eh?" After a moment Davy added, "Win or lose."

Jon couldn't speak. His eyes were wet, blinded.

Davy picked up his bag. Then he did something strange. He swung down and kissed Jon on the lips, for the first time, on his way out the door.

About Emma Donoghue

Emma Donoghue was born in Ireland and now lives in Canada. She is best known for her novels—*Stirfry, Hood,* and *Slammerkin*—but also writes plays, radio drama, and literary history. *Kissing the Witch*, her collection of reimagined fairy tales, was short-listed for a James Tiptree Award and named an ALA Popular Paperback for Young Adults in 2000. Emma Donoghue has contributed stories to several young adult anthologies. Her latest book is a collection of historical stories called *The Woman Who Gave Birth to Rabbits*. You can read more about her work by visiting her Web site at www.emmadonoghue.com.

" 'Team Men,' " she writes, "is a retelling of the Old Testament story of Saul, David, and Jonathan, but it was also inspired by memories of my first relationship, at convent school in Dublin in the 1980s. It was the very first sexual experience for both my girlfriend and me, and we were thrilled by it, but terrified at the prospect of being lesbians. Although we were never found out, our fear often made us lash out at each other. So I suppose this story is about love's attempt to flower within the tense hothouse environment of a team of any kind."

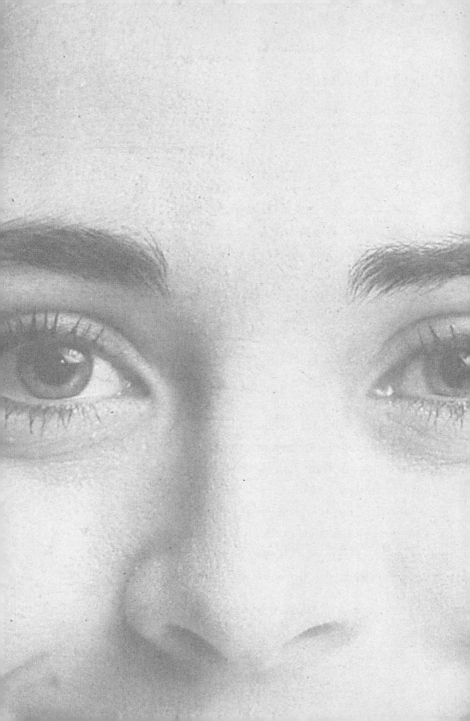

DAWN

RICH WALLACE

FOR TWO days I have been surrounded by lithely writhing dancers, intensely brilliant cellists and singers, and lyrical expressers of inner-city/rural/suburban angst and desire.

You may have heard of the Griffito Conference, a weeklong summer workshop for teenage poets, musicians, and dancers. It's sponsored by some giant corporation like Microsoft or the Republican Party.

I'm being cynical. It's sponsored by the Griffon Foundation, which is apparently a big deal in its own right.

They run contests and auditions in late winter to attract several dozen of us for a week of (this is from the brochure) "sharing, learning, experimentation, and growth in the idyllic setting of the lakeside Athenaeum Institution in western New York State."

I like words. But no way in hell do I belong here.

My English teacher (and track coach) badgered me to apply. He tells me I have a point of view, and I suppose I agree with him. When I write lyrics, which isn't often, I just write about what I'm going through after making a jerk of myself with a girl or feeling powerless and stupid after an argument with my father. And I don't go comparing myself to a wilted dandelion or using metaphors or that other shit; I just lay out the emotions and try to let you know what I'm saying instead of expecting you to interpret.

But I am way outclassed here. By everybody.

* * *

My mother dropped me off in Scranton early Sunday and I boarded a bus for Erie, six hours away. After a two-hour wait I took a second bus to Jamestown, New York, where I was picked up in a van and driven another half hour to the gates of the Institution, arriving dehydrated and nervous at dusk.

"We're so glad you're here, Ronny," said Mrs. Henderson, the gray-haired conference director, when I showed up at the dorm. "You missed dinner. You're in one of the singles—the rooms are tiny, but we hope there'll be as much interaction as possible." She brought her hands together in a sharp little clap, touching her fingertips to her chin. "You must be exhausted. Are you?"

I let my gym bag slip down off my shoulder and grabbed the handles. "I guess I'm okay. Thirsty, maybe."

She smiled. "We have bottles of water, lots of them, in that little room over there. In the fridge. Today we just get to know each other. At dinner, for example."

I started to say something about getting a bottle of water, but she was only taking a microsecond to breathe. She clapped her hands again and said, "Now, you-ou . . . are in room 2-H. It's a little musty. You don't have asthma or anything?"

"No. Not, uh . . . no."

"Then you'll be fine. So glad you're here. The other poets . . . it's a diverse group. Such sweet girls. And Ramon—he's from the Bahamas. Just four boys in the poetry group. Ten girls. You're not a smoker?"

"No. I run."

"We ask that you smoke outside. . . . So. You've arrived."

I nodded and pointed toward the stairs. "Up here?"

"Yes." She smiled tightly. "You'll be fine. Just fine."

On Monday morning they brought everyone together for an inspirational talk on creativity by some professor from Cornell. Then the dancers headed off for the dance hall, the musicians for the conservatory, and the poets stayed put in the dormitory conference room.

Jim, the guy running the poetry strand, is about thirty, with short dark hair and glasses. He teaches at Kenyon College. He read us a few of his poems—dense, self-absorbed, and pompously literate. Strange, because he's witty and cheerful, the type who probably plays volleyball at picnics. He was wearing a golf shirt and expensive sandals; most of us were in T-shirts and shorts. A few of the girls were in halters.

We did the usual getting-to-know-you exercise, going around the circle to state our name, place, interests, and hopes for the week.

Ramon likes MTV and women of all types. He considers himself a lyricist as much as a poet, "but what's the difference anyway? Nassau rocks; you must visit me there," he says.

Sue is Nebraskan, and her poems cover "horses, desires, and eating disorders." Molly is down from Toronto and writes about "eclectic stuff—Rivers. Rage. Ice cream." She giggles.

Dawn. From outside Boston. Stunning to look at. I'd have placed her in the dance group if I'd had to guess. "Tom Waits. The Pogues. Irwin Shaw—his stories more than the novels. Coffee, carrots, blueberries. Nat King Cole. Jack London. Anything by Toni Morrison or Annie Proulx." Her navel is pierced with a silver ring.

Twice back home I've given books to girls I was interested in. Salinger's *Nine Stories* to a smart-mouthed hurdler with nimble legs; *Cannery Row* to a girl I shared a joint with at a party. They both said things like "Wow, this looks great I can't wait to read it," and then never mentioned books, or reading, again.

I'm in the dark when it comes to women. Like anybody else I'm wanting physical release more than anything cerebral. Is it too much to ask for both in the same package? Maybe not. Maybe here.

My turn. I try to be funny. "I'm from this little hick town in Pennsylvania. Mostly I run track and cross country and play summer-league basketball. I read a lot of stuff. Magazines. A few novels. I get C's in English. My poems are simple and I've only written a few. I hang with my friends on Main Street and we bust each other's chops about zits and parents and masturbating. I'm a big TV watcher. A slug." I don't mention my batting average with women, which is zero.

They were all looking at me, of course, since I was speaking. But my eyes met Dawn's. She was smiling at me, looking interested. I hope I wasn't blushing.

*   *   *

Mrs. Henderson keeps stressing to us that the Foundation is eager to bring about cross-cultural and cross-discipline understanding, so we should strive to interact as artists, rather than poet to poet or clarinetist to oboe player. So we have assigned tables at dinner, and there are opportunities to bike or play basketball or dance recreationally after hours. Before dinner on Monday I played two-on-two basketball with Ramon and a couple of ballerinas. My teammate was Christina, who is leggy with short straight hair, big eyes, and plainly beautiful features. Also the high, muscled butt of the well-trained athlete. She sucks at basketball, though.

Ramon is a showman, making elaborate drives and behind-the-back passes that left his teammate, Tanya, in a state of amusement and confusion. We won, despite Christina, but neither girl seemed to notice how well I shoot jumpers. They were both intrigued by Ramon, who has an endless capacity to coyly suggest having sex without ever really bringing it up. "I *love* to drive the lane," he says after scooting past Christina for a layup. He was talking about swimming in the lake at night as I slipped away after the game.

After showering I went down to the cafeteria. My table included Sue, the Nebraskan poet; an instructor from the music school and two of his pupils; and, to my delight, Christina.

Jerry, the instructor, dominated the dinner conversation by telling about his recent trip to Europe. He was interesting and funny, but I'd rather have been flirting with Christina. She did not seem to be flirtatious, so I looked around and spotted Dawn at another table. She was talking to a musician.

I followed Christina out just for the hell of it. "Need to brush my teeth," she said, which I took as a dismissal. "Then maybe a walk by the lake."

"Sounds nice."

"Join me."

My heart began to race. "Uh . . . okay," I said. "I'll meet you right here."

I ran upstairs, brushed my teeth vigorously, gargled with mouthwash, and reapplied deodorant. Then I ran back down.

It was at least twenty minutes before she returned, and she had four other people with her, two of them guys.

We are not the only ones here this week, not at all. The Institution is a gated community that's bigger than the town I live in, and it's all tree-sheltered old homes and small inns and shops. Families come here for a week or a summer of swimming and boating. The symphony plays at night in a wooden amphitheater; there are lectures and classes on chess and philosophy and creative writing and religion. It all seems safe and white and sort of artificial, what with the gates and the wealth and the security patrol on bicycles. The grounds are about a half mile wide and three times that long, and everything slopes toward the water.

The lake was beautiful; the walk was boring. They were all

dancers, and the talk was entirely over my head. I said nine-teen words in the next ninety minutes and was relieved when we got back to the dorm.

This morning—Tuesday—we read poems we'd been told to bring with us. First a personal favorite from a published work, then one of our own for discussion. I read Gary Soto's "Profile in Rain," then what I think is probably my best, called "The Hour Before." It's about warming up for the district cross-country championships last year, the anguish you go through, afraid you'll fail, the heat building inside you, the growing calm as you focus and remember how hard you worked to get there.

Reading one of my poems in front of a dozen other writers is almost as nerve-inducing as racing.

Some of the other poets are truly amazing. Ramon, for all his cockiness and flash, reads an introspective poem about the beach at night after his father has left in drunkenness and anger, comparing the reflection of the moon on the water to the way he sees himself in his dad.

Melanie, a quiet girl from New Jersey, cracks us all up with a hilarious poem about getting dressed for a junior high dance.

At lunch I hesitate on the buffet line, pondering a choice of tuna salad or bologna. I opt for yogurt and several pieces of fruit. You can sit wherever you want at lunch, so I scan the room for a spot. Then I set my tray on the counter near the juices. As I'm filling a glass with fruit punch, I feel a knock against the back of my knee, and I tilt forward slightly and spill it on the counter.

"Hey," Dawn says, grinning at me.

"Hi. Was that you?"

She kind of flicks up her eyebrows. "Mmm-hmm."

"Thanks."

"You're welcome."

What a smile. She again becomes my immediate, intense priority. "Where are you sitting?" I ask.

"Right there," she says, pointing. "I saved you a spot."

I get a fresh glass of juice, shut my eyes for a second, and say a silent prayer of thanks. Then I join her at the table.

"They're bringing in a DJ tonight," she says.

"Really?"

"Yeah. You can dance, right?"

I roll my eyes. "Some."

"You must have strong legs," she says. "All that running."

"Yeah," I say. "I go fine when I'm moving in a straight line. Dancing is a different matter."

"I love to dance," she says. She beats out a rhythm on the table. "You ever do a poetry slam?"

"You mean like a reading?"

"No. Well, yeah. But a slam is physical, too. Very animated. You get up and perform your poems, like a storyteller. It's where poetry and muscle overlap." She flexes her biceps.

There's a tiny star tattooed on her shoulder. "I'm putting together a slam for Friday night. You're up for it, right?"

"Sure," I say, kind of tentative. Then I realize that no one knows me here; I can be anybody I want to be. "Definitely," I say with some authority. "I'll be there."

I squeeze in a workout before dinner, kind of a slow anticipatory run along the lake. No sense tiring out my legs. I think real hard about what to wear tonight, but I don't have many options. Shorts. Running shoes. The Adidas T-shirt, I suppose. It's clean.

Around nine I start looking for Dawn. I know I'll see her at the dance hall, but I'd like to meet up with her first, let people notice that we arrive together. But I don't find her. So I walk the hundred yards alone.

I see her right away, dancing with a group of girls. Her shirt is low-cut and her skin is glistening. The music is coming from a cheap little boom box, and there's no sign of a DJ. There are only about fifteen people in the room. I take a seat in a wooden folding chair.

After about four songs she comes over to me.

"What's going on?" I say.

"Nothing much," she says. "They said the friggin' DJ isn't going to show. What a rip."

"Yeah."

She gently grabs my arm. "Come on," she says, leading me toward a small stage on the other side of the room. There's a tiny booth there with a chest-high window. She opens a door on the side and we enter the booth.

"I can do this," she says.

There are two CD players, one on either side of the counter in front of the window, with a flat soundboard between them— knobs and lights and a stick for mixing the songs from the two CDs. She turns a couple of switches and leans over the microphone.

"Dawn and Ronny are in the house," she announces. "Brothers and sisters, let's crank it up."

She slips in something by a girl group and turns up the volume, then starts going through the CDs. There's a lot of classical stuff, of course, since this is the ballet hall. But there are about a dozen contemporary rock/dance-mix CDs and some greatest-hits collections: the Stones, Madonna, R.E.M.

"We'll be all right," she says. "We'll rock."

I catch on fast and work the CD player on the right. You get the track ready to go, then start it just as the left one is finishing. Dawn works the stick and does some smooth transitions. Before long there are at least thirty people dancing.

There's a lot of bumping around in the close quarters of a DJ booth, leaning over to pop out a disc, working the mix stick, reaching for CD cases, an intentional elbow to the biceps. We take turns drinking from a bottle of Sprite; I cap the bottle and shake it between sips, slowly releasing the carbon dioxide to make it flat.

"Quirky," she says.

"Tastes better," I say.

"Whatever."

"I know what I'm doing," I say. I burp too much if it hasn't been defizzed.

I reach in close when I hand the bottle to her. We dance in place. She lights a filtered Camel.

Ramon brings over a predictable CD. Dawn looks at it, pronounces it danceable. He leans into the booth, talking to her, making her laugh. He's smooth, he's polite, but you can tell he's thinking they'll be gettin' jiggy wit it later. Poet, my ass. She gives me a sly smile when he leaves.

There's a certain intimacy in her cigarette smoke, how she doesn't bother to turn her head but lets the barely visible stream envelop me. The pursing of her lips to release the smoke, the touching of her tongue to her teeth. The night goes on. We sip from a bottle of sneaked-in beer. I have to remind myself continually not to stare at that pocket of skin between her breasts, though her outfit is shouting at me to do so. It's saying Look, look closer. Don't even blink; it'll disappear.

The place starts clearing out after midnight, but we go on until one. We straighten up a little, turn off the equipment.

"We rocked," she says. "This is a permanent gig unless the DJ shows tomorrow." She bumps my thigh with her butt. "Let's go."

We head for the dorm and she's giddy and talkative, and she puts her hand on my shoulder. We stand outside and laugh a little, teasing, joking about how sanitized the Institution feels. I am drained of energy, but I won't be able to sleep. There is no supervision in the dorm; she could stay in my room. But I'm very patient. I'll wait until tomorrow. I've been waiting all my life.

I brush my teeth, cup water in my hands, and rinse. I pull my shirt over my head and press it against my face. A T-shirt is the best absorber of scents: her smoke, your sweat, and something else entirely, something spicy, something definite and permanent from Dawn. Something tangible to take to bed with me. Almost like sleeping with her.

I have a hard time concentrating during the Wednesday-morning poetry session, glancing over at Dawn, thinking about tonight. I blow off lunch and go down to the tiny pharmacy at Bellinger Plaza near the amphitheater for breath mints and condoms.

We break into pairs in the afternoon to try collaborative poems. I'm with Molly, the Canadian. She has developed a hopeless attraction to Julio, a deadpan wit from New Mexico with bushy black hair, three earrings, and large teeth. I confess that I'm hung up on Dawn (but I'm pretty confident about where that's leading). We decide on an ambiguous crush poem, one that could work in any combination of genders.

I let Molly do most of the work. She is self-deprecating and sweet, and aware of the great odds against her. Our group is ten females to four guys; the dance group is even more decidedly feminine. Only the musicians have a more or less equal ratio, so this is a terrific place to be a guy.

I turn inward in late afternoon, taking a longer run, stopping to stare at the lake and feel the blood pumping through my muscles. I take a hot, lengthy shower and stay quiet at dinner. I wave to Dawn but stay cool. Then I return to my room to read.

I wait until after nine-thirty to walk to the dance hall, hoping to create anticipation on her part. The place is much fuller tonight; the word must have gotten around. But there's a guy in the DJ booth, and he's older than any of us.

So we won't be in there tonight, but it's just as well. I'd rather dance with her out here. I'd rather be able to break away early.

She looks incredible. Dark halter top, short denim skirt, leather sandals, a choker of Navajo beads.

She finds me right away, touching my wrist. "How was your run?" she asks.

"Great," I say. "Invigorating." I say this suggestively. I can't help it. She is coy enough not to react yet.

"Where've you been?" she asks.

"Hanging out," I say. I jut my chin toward the DJ booth. "The professional showed up, huh?"

She shakes her head in faux disappointment. "Too bad," she says. "We kicked ass."

"Definitely," I say. "We're a hell of a team."

"It was fun."

"We're perfect together."

She nods, looks out at the dancers.

"We should get out there," I say, meaning the dance floor.

"Yeah," she says. "I'll be back."

She walks off toward the bathroom. I notice Molly talking to Julio, laughing on the other side of the room. And Ramon is dancing tight with Tanya, the ballerina he tried to seduce on the basketball court.

Dawn is gone a long time. I stick my head outside and find her smoking on the steps.

"Hey," I say.

"Hey."

"You all right?"

"Yeah. Just needed a smoke." She crushes it in the dirt and gets up to join me. We go in and start dancing. I guess she's okay.

The dancing feels awkward at first, and she's looking around instead of at me. But she loosens up after a couple of songs, and soon we're laughing and bumping and working up a sweat.

We leave at midnight and head for the lake. The grounds are dark and quiet, and the sky is a mass of stars between the treetops.

"Great night," she says, taking my hand. "Look at the Dipper. It's so huge."

We take a seat on a dock, the water lapping all around us, smelling cool and deep and weedy.

"I could stay here all night," she says, closing her eyes and inhaling.

"Yeah." This seems to be working, so I say, "I'd love to see the crack of dawn," which is so damn clever I can't believe I said it. I guess she didn't hear me.

We're quiet for a few minutes. When she speaks, it's just above a whisper. "I try to kill a whole night when I can, just letting it wash over me. Not trying to think or even move much. We forget that there's two sides to the day."

"We can stay up," I say. "We can lie on this dock until dawn comes."

This time she gives me what people refer to as a sidelong glance. There's a slight little twitch at the corner of her mouth while she ponders whether that was Freudian or intentional. That could be a smile starting, so I push it further and say, "Or I do."

The twitch becomes a full-fledged sneer, and she turns away with a single word: "Asshole."

She sits forward now, staring at the lake, then fumbles in her pocket for a cigarette. She smokes it sort of disdainfully, if you can picture that. When the smoke is over, she stands up. "We'd better get back."

My God, I'm a shithead.

Thursday is painful. I don't even remember the sessions. I don't participate except when I'm called on.

I say screw dinner and walk over to Bellinger Plaza, getting a turkey-and-what-looks-like-seaweed sandwich on yuppie bread made of cornhusks and acorn chips. I have no appetite anyway. Needless to say, Dawn avoided me. Needless to say, this entire week has been an embarrassment.

I walk for three hours, making loops around the perimeter of the Institution. When I'm tired enough, I walk past the dance hall, which is not crowded but is still pumping out music.

Tomorrow this will be over. Saturday I'll take two buses. Sunday night I'll be back on Main Street. Monday I'll begin training for the fall.

I am not an artist. Muscle can beat art. Muscle can rip through a painting and shatter a sculpture and splash through a reflection in the moonlight.

Muscle kicks ass. It means something.

*   *   *

Friday in class Molly reads "our" poem aloud:

Unstraightened hair
Pulled back but bushy
Piled high
Glossy
Strands unwinding
Reaching
Dark
Rich and black
Unstraightened
Unreachable
Unrequited
Unreal

The class applauds. We applaud for all the poems.

Dawn says, "Don't forget the slam tonight, everybody. Three minutes apiece before the dance. Tell everybody from the other groups about it."

I feel a little better. Class is over. I walk out alone.

"You coming tonight?" she says from behind me.

I turn. "Sure."

She nods, hesitates, walks back inside. "See you there."

It goes well. Dawn is great. Molly, too. I do two quick poems. I start with "Waiting for You in the Produce Aisle," which I figure will get a laugh.

Jenny, Jenny, Jenny
I would spend a penny
for every second in your arms . . .
not to exceed twenty-five dollars.

That's the whole poem. It gets a decent reaction. I follow it with "The Hour Before." I close my eyes halfway through, stop trying to perform. I just say it, slow and steady, and I feel it again. The way I felt when I wrote it.

I will fail again
If not this time, then another
And the failure will propel me
And I'll triumph once again.

That is a poem that is too personal to share, too preachy and unrefined. But I've given it two audiences this week. Maybe that will help me revise it.

The dance is wild, a release and a celebration for most. I stay to the side, still wounded. Dawn comes up to me later, unraveled and perspiring. She stands there. I stand there. We stand there.

"A bit of advice," she finally says, "since you seem like a decent guy." She's not exactly looking at me, just kind of beyond me toward the dancers. "You could have had me." This is straight talk—no blushed whispering for her. "It would have taken another night or two, and it would have been my choice, not yours. But it would have happened if you'd let it. It would have happened."

The next morning I pack my gym bag and hustle downstairs for my ride into Jamestown. Mrs. Henderson shakes my hand and tells me again how wonderful it was to have me. Ramon is packed and waiting. He shakes my hand, says I must come see him during Carnival.

Dawn is there too. She comes over and gently smacks my arm.

I nod for a few seconds, thinking what to say. Sorry seems stupid, so I say thanks instead.

"Yeah," she says. "Okay."

"I'm glad I was here," I say. "It's been something."

The van pulls in. I pick up my bag. I look back at Dawn. I move forward.

I'll spend today on buses; I'll spend tomorrow resting. Tomorrow night I'll go for a long, long run. Through town. Out of town. In the dark, in the cool, in the night.

I'll run so far that the night will wash over me.

I'll run so far I'll reach daylight.

ABOUT RICH WALLACE

Rich Wallace is the acclaimed author of three books set in tiny Sturbridge, Pennsylvania. His first, *Wrestling Sturbridge*, was named an ALA Top Ten Book for Young Adults and an ALA Quick Pick and was followed by *Shots on Goal*. His latest, *Playing Without the Ball*, was chosen by the ALA as one of its Best Books for Young Adults. Rich is also a senior editor at *Highlights for Children* magazine.

Rich Wallace writes, "Unfortunately, unrequited desire was a near daily occurrence for me as a teenager. I have mined several of the worst moments already for scenes in my novels. A frequently vomiting girlfriend, for example, inspired a scene in *Shots on Goal*. The passage in *Wrestling Sturbridge* about the high school newspaper's gossip column actually happened to me too. My relationship with my first girlfriend ended rather pathetically (actually, it had started pathetically and continued that way, so the ending was fitting). Anyway, I thought I was winning her back because she was nice enough not to hang up on me when I called every day for a couple weeks. Then 'RW—Leave me alone!' in black-and-white in the school newspaper. And it was done."

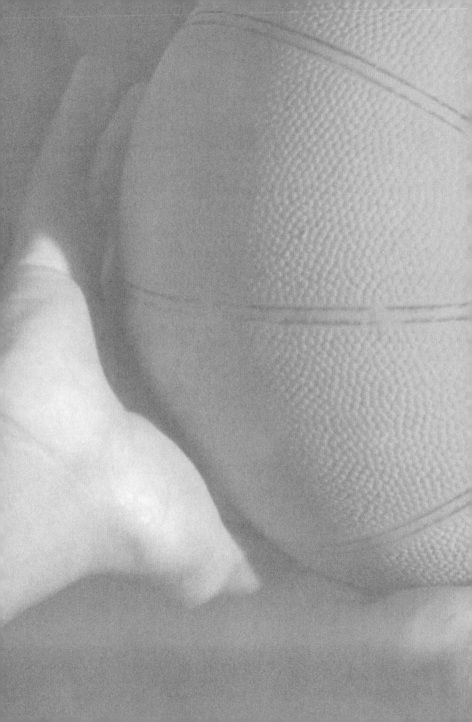

A KIND OF MUSIC

ANGELA JOHNSON

I ALWAYS thought I felt good in my own skin.
Never thought I'd care what I looked like to
someone else.
But when Tank won horse, then played
a pickup game and afterward poured his
Coke all over himself and looked across the
court at me like I was something new . . .
Something sweet.
Something good in my skin.
We just had to be.

Afterward my best friend, Nikki,
laughed,
elbowed me, and whispered,
"Girl, he sure is fine."

And he was.

So when he walked over and said,
"I'm Tank, what's your name?"

And I just looked at him, then fell
off the hood of Nikki's car.
And when he laughed until he cried and I wanted to be
    in his skin—

I knew. I just knew.

*   *   *

Starr F. says that Tank only dates
cheerleaders.
And even though I am one . . . (hmm . . .) I wonder . . .

He gave me a ride on the back of his
motorcycle, doing wheelies past my mom's
best friend's house on a too hot evening.

I thought I would die.
(On the bike, and when my mom found out and got
her hands on me.)

Will any of it matter?
How can I love somebody who will only
date cheerleaders? (If that's really true.)

What if I get caught smoking in the bathroom
or doing Jell-O shots on the football field and
get kicked off the squad?

Where would that leave me?

*   *   *

Tank can't sing.
But he tries to.
We got kicked out of the theater when he kept
singing the theme song to the movie.

He said he couldn't get it out of his head.

The manager said he was not asking us to leave because
   of the singing,
but because the singing was bad.

It is bad, but it makes me hold on to his hand
hard when we walk out into the parking lot with
nothing to do for two hours.

So we sing. We sit on top of the car on this long stretch
   of road
down from the old mills and sing
anything we can think of.

Tank doesn't care how he sounds and after a while
I lean against him, warm.
And with his arms around me,
it's like singing with an angel.

*   *   *

I'm not allowed to call Tank
my boyfriend.
It makes my mom crazy and she's not somebody
you want to get crazy.

I'm not allowed to be out past nine on school nights.
Not past eleven on weekends.
My time out got cut down when I got a boyfriend.

My mom pays more attention to me and asks
me if I need tampons all the time.
Havin' a lot of quality time with my mom lately.

Tank comes over and makes my mom even crazier
by trying to get her to like him.
She does, but hates herself for it.

Tank talks about how he wants to teach school
and make everything better.
It makes my mom crazy still 'cause she can't
stand that I picked somebody who doesn't
look like a future serial killer.

Don't have to call Tank boyfriend.
Don't have to say anything to him at all
sometimes.

Just watch him and say nothing at all.

*   *   *

Nikki asks me when me and Tank are finally
going to do it.
And I say with my arms folded across my chest,
"Do what?"

I get so mad and almost fall off
the platforms I stole on a dare from
the shoe store down the street.

Nikki blows a big-ass bubble and says,
"Sex. Make love. Screw. Do it!"

I keep wondering when my friends are going
to get out of my face about me being a virgin.

They say virgin like I'm drowning puppies
in the basement of their houses.

Virgin.

They say it like it's spit on all of them.

Virgin.

*   *   *

It's a good thing
Tank doesn't go to my
school or we'd probably
end up against lockers with tongues
down each other's throats like
some of my friends.

I figure it's safe sex.

The safest sex there ever could be is
not being in the same building with your boyfriend.

I got hundreds of people and a highway between
me and Tank.

His school on one side of the highway.
Mine on the other.

It's a good thing Tank knows lockers
aren't my thing.
It's okay that he knows I want him,
but not necessarily in front of everybody.

Across the highway on the other
side,
he knows I want him. . . .

*   *   *

He doesn't say . . .
"You would if you loved me."

He doesn't say . . .
"We'll love each other even more."

He doesn't say . . .
"I don't know what's going to happen if
I can't have you."

I think . . .
I love him.

I think . . .
I'll love him even more.

I think . . .
I don't know what's going to happen if
I can't have him.

*   *   *

Condoms.
There are ribbed ones.
Blue and all-different-colored ones.
There are lubricated and even ones made
for women.

Lined up in neat zigzaggy rows
on the drugstore shelf.

Looking at me and daring me not to buy
every last one that I can.

I have to 'cause Starr F. says the waiting room
in the women's clinic has old magazines
and you have to fill out a five-thousand-word
questionnaire. (Nikki says she's lying.)

And if you're our age, you have to get a fake ID to get
   it done.

I grab a handful of condoms 'cause I've been watching
girls younger than me push strollers
and change diapers in the bathroom at
football games with their school jackets on the
floor.

No glamour in stretch marks,
so I pick the ribbed ones and wonder what ribbed means
anyway.

*   *   *

There are all kinds of music you can kiss to.

I like anything slow that lets you take your time and
really feel everything around you.
And your body gets warm and melting on the spot.

Tank likes to listen to hip-hop 'cause it's always a
dance with him. He kisses like he's starting a dance
    marathon.
Everything could go on for hours and has to keep a beat.

I'm slow R&B.

Tank is funky hip-hop.

It is a kind of music when you are touching each other
and feeling warm and soft.

But when you get past the touching parts and go on—
there doesn't have to be any music playing anywhere
at all.

*   *   *

Nikki says,
"So, how was it?"

I look at her, shrug, and wonder if the
girl has some sort of radar when it comes to
my sex life.

"Fine," I say.

"Do you love him more?" she asks.

I shrug again and think how I slept like a baby
last night after Tank dropped me off at home.

I think about how he smelled of sweet soap and boy.

I think about how he was shy and I wasn't as shy as
I thought I would be.

I remember how his eyes welled up with tears after the
motion and heavy sweet breathing was over.

I remember how I kept thinking it all must be
a dream until Tank's tears spilled on me
and I held him tighter than I ever had before.

I walk away from Nikki, smiling and silent.

*   *   *

When I wake up, there is a big old box
of condoms on my bedside table and a copy of
Our Bodies, Ourselves.

I can't even go to breakfast and face my mom.

It isn't because she knows about me and Tank.
It isn't because I'm embarrassed about what I'm doing.

I figure something has changed between
me and my mom.

Will she see me different? Adult?

I'm not ready for that.

I don't want anything to change. . . .

So I sit here worried in my room, eating a bag of stale
    chips, until
I hear her yelling that I messed the kitchen up so bad
    with Nikki the other
night making macaroni and cheese she thinks we both
    need baby
dropcloths stapled to our shoes.

I smile, put the condoms in my nightstand and the book
on my desk, then head down to breakfast.

*   *   *

I beat Tank playing horse on the courts yesterday.

Pure and simple.
Smooth and easy.

He'd said he couldn't love any girl who couldn't
shoot hoops.

So since I always could, I make sure I beat him
anytime I get the chance.

It always makes him smile when I do.

I look at him and know why I want to be near him.
Beside him.
Always close to him.

He is something good. Something sweet.

And when we are leaning against the metal fence
watching other games and one of his friends says in
a loud whisper to him,
"She's fine, man."

I whisper in the other ear,
"How did you know?"

And Tank just says,
"I knew. I just knew."

About Angela Johnson

A winner of the Lee Bennett Hopkins Poetry Award, the Ezra Jack Keats New Writer Award, and the PEN/Norma Klein New Writer Award, Angela Johnson writes poetry, picture books, short stories, and novels. Her acclaimed novels for young adults include *Gone from Home*, *Humming Whispers*, *Songs of Faith*, and two Coretta Scott King Award winners, *Toning the Sweep* and *Heaven*.

"When I was fourteen, I used to dream that I'd grow up to be a passionate writer, moody and bold, who lived on the beach (which I only came close to when my basement plumbing exploded during a particularly cold winter). Down the beach would be an artist with an unpronounceable name who would paint me and love everything I wrote. I did not dream that I'd watch soaps all day, eat too much fried food, and annoy my friends about going out to lunch when I can't write a thing. Uncombed hair, mismatched socks, and an oversized T-shirt with coffee stains down front was not how I imagined my life as a writer.

"In the end I live in a Midwestern town about two blocks from a river's edge, where I secretly still look for that artist. Maybe his plumbing exploded too, and he's stuck in his basement. . . ."

About The Editor

Cathy Young is the creator of Favorite Teenage Angstbooks, a popular Web site that celebrates teen angst, personal discovery, and great young adult literature. She lives in the Pacific Northwest. Visit her Web site at: www.grouchy.com/angst and write to her at cathy@grouchy.com.